MINA BETH LU AND THE MUSICAL SCORE

TWISTED: MODERN-DAY FAIRY TALES WITH A TWIST

EVIE RALSTON

DLG TWISTED STORIES

FAIRY TALES WITH A TWIST OF HORROR

The Swine Huntress & the Three Brothers

Lilithe Torin-Godderd and the Woodcutter

FAIRY TALES WITH A TWIST OF FANTASY

Sacha Shepperd Ninette and the Dark Night

Jack Dante LaBanks and the BeanStalk

Mina Beth Lu and the Musical Score

FAIRY TALES WITH A TWIST OF SCI-FI

Adanya Tebbet-Theus and the Dark Mask

Mina Beth Lu and the Musical Score is a modern-day twist to Thumbelina.

Music speaks to her heart, body, and soul—when lost in a composition, she's free to be herself.

Mina Beth Lu yearns to compose and play in a prestigious orchestra. But when selected for a performance position, she soon finds herself evading the clutches of those who seek to blackmail her into marriage and harness her musical ability for themselves.

Nico Strata, scarred by the death of his parents, meets the girl of his dreams. But she's kidnapped before he can profess his love to her. While searching for her, he grows emotionally and learns all about hope and dreams with the help of a few close friends.

Dedicated to readers of classic fairy tales. May you each find that special someone who makes your heart flutter, your body come alive, and your soul sing.

Special thanks to my family and friends. Your encouragement means the world to me.

Mina Beth Lu and the Musical Score
Twisted: Modern-Day Fairy Tales with a Twist
COPYRIGHT©2020
Evie Ralston
Cover Design by Wren Taylor

Published in the United States of America by:

DLG Publishing Partners

San Antonio, TX 78217

www.DLGPublishingPartners.com

The publisher does not have any control over and does not assume any responsibility for author or third-party websites or their content.

CONTENTS

Mina Beth Lu

A bird chirped in auto play.

Mina Beth Lu slid her hands under her pillow and sandwiched both ears. Extra work shifts at the call center, and triple practice sessions in the orchestra soundproof rooms, had finally caught up with her.

Ugh. Can't a girl catch a few Zs before class? Just five more minutes, that's all.

Birds chirped at different intervals—some sharp, some flat—and wings flapped.

Slowly, and with much regret, Mina still teetering on the edge of sleep and consciousness, begun to wake.

Something isn't right in the room—was it a hunch, a feeling, a thought? She couldn't pinpoint exactly what made her feel like this. Reluctantly, she released the pillow, opened her eyes, then pulled the covers down from around her head.

Sunlight bathed the room, blinding her.

Oh, geez. What time is it?

She struggled to shrug off the last remaining strings of

sleep. Sliding a hand fromm underneath the warmth of the covers, she felt around for her phone.

Where is that damn thing?

Chirp. Chirp. Chirp.

Through eyes squinted against the light, Mina scanned the room, then her phone. It was then she realized her mistake.

Ten o'clock in the morning. She tossed the covers back and sprung from the bed.

"I'm gonna be late."

The shaggy fibers of the rug next to her bed smooched between her toes—or squished, she wasn't sure which of the two it was yet. She took two steps, then stopped to visually follow a shadow darting across her room.

What the hell is that?

She continued to follow the erratic pattern of the shadow, which, if she was correct, was about to dive-bomb the area she stood in.

Chirp. Chirp. Chirp.

Her brain raced to process the incoming information. She ducked just in time, but the flying squatter buzzed by her head low enough, she heard the flutter of wings up close and personal.

"Great. Just what I needed today." Another step, and she got all the confirmation she needed.

Yep. That'd be a squish.

She peered at her feet and squeezed the wet fibers of the soaked rug between her toes.

A stormed had blown through the area last night. She had opened the blind and window for a bit of fresh air, and to allow the calming sounds of the rain hitting the tree just outside the window, to calm her nerves. But, evidently, it did more that. The rain had lulled her to sleep and came inside uninvited.

"Ugh, not today." She took in the damage.

At first, she worried the rainwater had reached the other side of the room, which was empty at the moment, but wouldn't stay that way for long. A new girl assigned to the bed hadn't moved in yet.

The rain had barely touched the floor on the other side of the room, and after a quick swipe of the plastic-covered mattress with a paper towel, the visible mess was gone.

Mina Beth's side of the room, closer to the open window, was an absolute mess.

Her suitcase sat open on the floor where she had left it the night before, having thought she would have time later, over the next few days—after auditions—to unpack the rest of her things.

Mina patted her hand against her quilt—soaked all the way through. She wondered why the wet mess hadn't woke her up. She peeled the wet layers back until she came across dry fabric.

The water hadn't gotten all the way to where Mina had slept, thanks to the sleeping bag under her comforter.

At least the bed's dry, the top blanket, not so much.

She cast a glance at the opened suitcase under the window and sighed. Kneeling, she sifted through layer after layer of damp clothing, hoping to find something dry at the bottom. But even those garments were just a little too damp to consider wearing in the upper fifties.

Mina sat on her knees, feeling lost, and checked her phone. She had missed the early morning auditions, but she still had an hour before class, which might be enough time to put something in the dryer for a few minutes. She rummaged around in her unpacked boxes for the roll of quarters she had brought with her.

Think. If you were quarters, where would you be?

The door to her room swung open hard enough to slam against the wall.

"Mina Beth Lu?" A female voice with a southern drawl boomed in the room. "Meet your new roommate."

Mina turned and looked at the girl in the doorway. Her wide smile fell as soon as she took in the room's state.

"Yes," said Mina Beth. "I'm so sorry about the mess, I can explain . . ."

"Is everything okay? It looks like it rained in here." She took a step into the room and looked around at the small puddles that had formed on Mina's desk, the windowsill, in the trashcan, on the chair, the floor, and the carpet. "Sorry, I'm being rude." She extended a hand. "I'm Autumn, your roommate."

"Autumn." Warmth spread over Mina's neck and face. "It's nice to meet you, and again, I'm so sorry. I left the window open last night, and I just woke up a few minutes ago. I don't know what to say."

"It's okay. You don't have to apologize. Do you need any help to clean? The three of us together could probably get this all fixed up in no time at all."

"Three?" Surprised, Mina looked past Autumn and saw someone standing behind her.

"Hey," a tenor voice said. "Sorry, lurking back here." He waved.

Autumn took a few steps in the room, allowing the person behind her to come into the light.

"I'm Nico." He locked eyes with her for a moment, then cracked a grin.

Loose curls hugged his head, and long, dark lashes made the blue of his irises pop.

Mina, suddenly aware of what she must looked like, standing in the middle of her soggy room in her fluffy pajamas with unbrushed hair and teeth, wished she could hit a rest button.

"What can we do to help?" Autumn wrapped her arm

through Nico's and pulled him next to her. "We're at your command."

Mina couldn't help but feel a pang in her chest, and a tad on the embarrassed side, for having found Nico attractive. She didn't want to step on anyone's toes, especially someone who she would have to live closely with for the next semester or two or three.

Regardless, she knew she didn't have time for a relationship. She had to overload her courses this semester to graduate on time, and even one failed grade would cost her another semester's worth of bills.

"Sorry I've got all my stuff in the way." Mina laughed, trying to shake off her nerves. "I have class in less than thirty minutes, so I've got to rush out soon, but I'll push all my stuff into a corner so you have more space."

"Hey, don't worry about it. I don't have all that much with me. Plus, I'll have Nico here helping me. It's okay if he's in the room, right?"

Mina turned her head to hide the slight blush warming her face. "Of course, it's fine." She pushed her plastic boxes underneath her bed, pausing when she got to her suitcase.

"Do you want us to wait outside for a minute while you get ready for class?" Autumn asked.

"No, it should be fine. I'll change in the bathroom." Mina realized she no longer had enough time to run to the laundry room before class. "Well, once I can find something dry to wear."

"I have some stuff you can borrow." Autumn pulled a suitcase into the room before Mina could reply. She set it on the ground and unzipped it. "Pick anything you want, and just return it once you have time to sort out your stuff."

Usually, Mina would be hesitant to accept a favor from someone she had just met, but she checked the time on her phone and knew she had no other options. She quickly grabbed a pair of jeans and a t-shirt from her roommate's suitcase, confirmed they were okay choices, and then ran to the bathroom to change.

In less than two minutes, Mina was dressed. She ran out the door to catch the bus across campus.

The wind blew a few brown leaves across the sidewalk, and Mina crunched each one under her feet as she walked. The summer still lingered in the hot air, but fall was just a few weeks away.

Mina looked at the sky and smiled, thinking about how much bluer it would look soon, when the trees turned orange and red.

A block away from the bus stop, she noticed the time and walked faster. As Mina got closer to the crosswalk, she looked up toward the street, catching sight of the bus, slowing pulling in to stop.

Dammit. She swore under her breath, then picked up her pace to a steady jog. Her violin case, held snug to her body, remained nearly motionless, but her pack with books slammed against her back, bruising a few ribs.

Deep down, she knew she was still too far away to make it. She was always running late, but usually tiptoed into class before they had gotten started. With the bus gone, she was better off walking, rather than trying her luck at waiting for the next one. With each step she took, Mina went over what she could tell the orchestra director when she showed up late. Hopefully, he would believe her when she explained what had happened.

It was Mina's third year in college, and she had worked hard to graduate early. But that all depended on her being able to pass this class. She had never met Director Harris before—the varsity instructor—and the rumor in the music department was that he was a tough critic and didn't tolerate lazy students. She even knew of one or two people kicked out for being late too many days in a row, which always seemed to be Mina's routine.

Her boots splashed through puddles as she hurried along, sending muddy drops of water onto the cuffed legs of her roommate's jeans.

Mina thought about the ways she could repay Autumn for her kindness, but she wasn't even sure what Autumn liked. Regardless, it would have to wait until later.

2

Nico Fratelli

Nico watched Mina leave before he turned to look around Autumn's new dorm. He stepped on a puddle that had gathered in the middle of the room, testing how much water was actually in the carpet.

"This will take some work." He turned to Autumn, who nodded.

"I've got some towels in one of those boxes there." Autumn pointed out into the hallway where the rest of her belongings lined the wall. "But I don't think it'll be enough."

"Well, we better get started then."

He helped her lay out the towels on the dampest parts of the floor, then walked over them, letting the pressure of his body weight squish the water out of the carpet and into the towels.

Phone in hand, he drafted a message to his uncle.

"Who ya sexting?" Autumn took a wet towel to the tub to wring out.

"No one. What do you take me for? I asked to borrow the shop vac from the store."

"You know I'm joking, right?" She sat on the side of the tub-shower combo "What'd your uncle say?"

"Said he'll be here in two shakes of a lamb's tail."

Autumn peeked out from around the bathroom door. "Where does he get those crazy phrases from? It's like he's a walking encyclopedia of cliches and old sayings."

"Yeah. That's one he likes to say a lot."

"Well, it sounds cute on one hand, and well, rather disturbing on the other."

"If you bag these up, my aunt will wash them." Nico dropped another towel in the tub. "You can pick them up after dinner." He walked out of the bathroom and checked the seal of the window. "And you're coming tonight, or I won't hear the end of it."

"Fine." She stepped out into the hall, then returned with a roll of brown, industrial paper towels cradled in her arms.

"Where did you get those from?"

"The janitor's closet in the hall—top shelf."

"Sweet." He waved to her. "Tear me off a bundle."

Autumn went around the room with the roll she had stolen from the bathroom, wadding up handfuls and wiping down the furniture and walls.

"Where's my girl?" Uncle Henry's voice boomed from outside the room.

"I'm in here." A smile danced across Autumn's lips. "Thanks for letting Nico use your car. It was way better than taking the bus. It would've been a seven hour ride—or longer —from my house."

"Glad to hear it, and much safer for a young lady." Nico's uncle entered the room: shop vac and tubing in one hand, and a wicker picnic basket with a handle in the other. "Now, I come bearing gifts."

"Oh, I'm starvin'." Autumn dropped the half-used roll of paper towels on the bed. "Are there some goodies in there?"

"You know there are." Henry winked at Autumn, then unburdened his hands. "When she found out you were comin' yesterday, she stayed up baking Snickerdoodles last night." He patted his belly. "And let me tell ya, they're good as always."

"Thanks for bringing the vacuum." Nico fit the pieces together, then plugged it in.

His uncle walked the room, assessing the damage. Taking turns, Nico and Henry sucked rainwater out of the carpet.

When they finished, the room only looked slightly better, but it still needed some work before Autumn could call it home, of that, he was certain.

"Well, I better get back to the music store." Uncle Henry gathered the shop vac and its supplies. "Your aunt's holding down the fort, and you know how she haggles prices . . ."

"Haggles, she gives stuff away." Nico chuckled.

"Exactly." Henry hugged Autumn, then gave Nico a nod. "I will see you both at the dinner table tonight. We're havin' meatloaf and all the trimmings."

"I know. I know." Autumn rolled her eyes. "Nico told me."

Henry walked out into the hall, leaving Nico and Autumn alone in the room.

"Well, at least the carpet doesn't make any squishing noises when I walk over it now." Nico shrugged, knowing that the rest would just have to air dry. "I think it's time for a break."

Autumn sat on her desk, resting her feet on the seat of the chair, and eating a Snickerdoodle.

"Give me one of those before you eat them all." Nico hopped onto her lofted bed, and the plastic of the bare mattress crinkled under his weight.

They sat in silence, eating the contents of the picnic

basket: turkey sub sandwiches, grapes, cheese sticks, apples, and more Snickerdoodles.

Nico rubbed the back of his neck. All the time he'd spent behind the wheel of his uncle's car the past two days had caught up to him. Five hours yesterday, driving to pick Autumn up only to drive her around to find things at the last minute, and then five more hours this morning to bring her to the campus. And now, he's spent half the day cleaning.

"Hey, I gotta call my mom. She's nesting again." Autumn sighed. "The woman is a mess without me. She needs a kitten, puppy, something to nurture."

"Tell her I said hello."

"Will do." Autumn stepped out into the hall. "She wants me to do a live call for a tour, so this could take a while."

"No problem. I can entertain myself." He waved her off, then watched until she disappeared around the corner.

Nico stared absently across the room, then grabbed the first of many boxes from the hall, and then retrieved the rest of her things from the car.

Thirty minutes later, Autumn walked into the room and looked at Nico. Her eyebrows furrowed.

"Why are you looking at me like that?" Nico sat on the edge of Autumn's loft.

"What are you looking at?" Autumn's eyes went to where Nico had been staring. "Ew, are you looking at Mina's stuff? Nico, are you being a creep?" Autumn laughed.

Nico blushed. He hadn't realized it, but he had been absently staring at the contents of Mina's suitcase.

"I am not! And there's nothing in there that would make me a creeper."

"It's creepy. You know you looking at all her 'unmentionables' as my mother or your aunt would say."

"It was an accident, I didn't realize . . ." Heat traveled up his neck and over his face. Hell, even his ears got hot, so he knew he was bright red. "Wait. I was staring off, not ogling her 'unmentionables.'"

"Yeah, whatever." Autumn laughed. "Wanna help me grab the rest of my stuff from the car?"

"Got it already."

"Then you can help me unpack." She shot him an animated grin. "Or are you gonna stare at my stuff, too?"

"Yeah, you wish."

"Ha. You're not my type, anyway." Autumn walked past him and playfully shoved him, and he stumbled into the wall, overdramatizing the movement.

"Ouch, Autumn. We've talked about this. You're stronger than you think." Nico rubbed his back where he had hit the wall behind him and pretended to pout.

"When we were kids, I felt bad, but now that you're twice as big as me, you can't complain anymore." Autumn slid a box to the middle of the floor, then started picking at the edges of the tape to open it.

"That's what you think." Nico hopped down from the bed and grabbed another box, opening it for her. "If I called your mom and told her you still push me around, she'd come right over with a box of cookies."

"If you called my mom and told her anything at all, she'd come over with a box of cookies for you and tissues to wipe your tears." Autumn ripped the tape off the box and unpacked books onto her desk.

Nico went back to the stacked boxes. He opened the ones on top, and found her bedding. "You what this on your bed now or later."

"Knock yourself out." Autumn was still bent over the box at her desk, slowly taking things out and organizing her books by color. "I'm not gonna stop ya if ya want to make my bed."

Once he made the bed, Nico dug into one of the medium-sized boxes, which was full of small printed-out posters and pictures of Autumn with friends and family.

"Speaking of being kids." Nico held up one picture for Autumn to get a better view. It was a photo of the two of them on Halloween, when Autumn was six and Nico seven.

"Cute, right? I found it in a box in my mom's closet over summer." Autumn stopped unpacking for a moment and took the picture from Nico's outstretched hand. "Just look at your little froggy costume my Mom made." She grinned. "Adorable."

"Well, I can't believe your mom ever got you to dress up like a little princess." Nico laughed.

Autumn never wore dresses and hated any kind of formal clothing. And with her mother's profession, a clothing designer, you'd think she'd beg to wear all the latest trends.

"What's the point of being uncomfortable?" She smacked her denim-covered thighs. "Jeans and tank tops, that's what I'm all about and an occasional oversized sweater in the winter.

"Man, she was so excited that Halloween."

"Tell me about it. She'd still dress me if she could. I'm sure she'd even put you in a dress if she thought you'd let her."

"You need to get more female friends. Not for yourself, specifically, but for your mother's sake. That way, she could play dress up."

"Honestly, that's not a bad idea. If I have more female friends. My mom has someone to sew dresses for—everyone wins."

"What about Mina?" Nico tried his best to keep his voice casual. If Autumn became close with Mina, it would give him more chances to see her.

"Yeah, she seems nice. I only talked to her for like a minute, though. I don't know what she's really like. Or if she's the girly type. I only saw her in jammies."

"Yeah, but they had little lace flower things, like—" Nico

rested a hand on his shoulder, "—right here. And that quilt, it's very floral."

"Liking flowers doesn't mean you're girly, Nico. But yeah, I get the point." Autumn reached into the next box in the work line and set more books on the shelf. "Wait." She gave him a side-eyed look. "Why do you have such an excellent memory of my roommate's jammies?"

"Can we talk about how you're twenty-one and still say 'jammies'?"

"That's a deflection. You're deflecting. Now, answer the question."

"Oh, wow, look at all these boxes. We should really focus on unpacking these, huh?"

Autumn glanced at her watch, sighed, and then looked around. "Man, we spent so much time cleaning the room, that I've barely gotten around to unpacking. And my first class starts tomorrow morning."

"But at least now, you know it's clean."

"I guess you're right. You've got work soon, and I need your free labor, or else I don't think I'll ever finish unpacking."

"Fantastic. Let me know what you need help with. As long as I don't have to answer any prying questions." Nico sat on the floor, peeling the tape off the rest of the boxes.

3

Mina Beth Lu

Mina looked up at Lewis Hall, the music building she had spent countless hours in over the last three years. But even that familiar sight wasn't able to comfort her. She walked into the building, overly conscious of her wet boots squelching on the speckled linoleum floor. A tremor shook her knees, and the rest of her body trembled in response.

The old, rusty door made a high-pitched scraping sound. The director immediately cut off the orchestra, and the practice hall went silent.

Mina could almost hear her frightened heartbeat, and she continued her uneasy walk to her assigned musical slot and dropped off her items.

Without turning around, Harris addressed the orchestra. "This must be Mina Beth Lu."

Mina, though shaking, made her way onto the stage, then searched for an empty seat. It seemed like everyone had assigned positions already.

Is it possible, the words swirled in her mind, crashing around. Did I miss the placement auditions entirely?

"Miss Lu, would you care to explain to us why you're late?" The director's voice boomed on stage.

She took a deep breath, then sighed. "It rained inside my room last night."

"It *rained* inside your room?" Harris laughed. "Please, enlighten the class. How does one encounter rain in a room?"

Mina looked over to the rest of the students in the orchestra for support, but no one would make eye contact with her. She didn't even recognize many people in the seated and wasn't close with the ones she did. There wasn't anyone to vouch for her or be a character witness if it came to that.

"N-not inside my room, exactly. Sorry. I left the window open overnight, and when I woke up, there was water everywhere. I'm sorry." She sucked air into her lungs, preparing to rattle off more of the story. "I cleaned it the best I could, borrowed dry clothes from my new roommate, and ran to the bus stop, but missed it. Honestly, I came as fast as I could."

Harris turned to face her, and his expression shifted in a way that Mina didn't understand. "Well, just make sure it doesn't happen again." He turned back to look at the rest of the orchestra. "I don't tolerate tardiness, and I won't accept any excuses. When you're late, you waste my time, and the time of your peers."

"Yes, Sir," mumbled Mina, close to tears. "Sorry."

"Just remember for next time. There's still almost an hour left in class. Take a seat over there"—he pointed to an empty chair along the wall—"and play third. You can do your formal placement audition after class."

"Yes, Sir." Mina nodded and quickly took a seat. The person she sat next to shifted his music stand, so she could read along. The student, Tyler, Toby, or Taylor, she couldn't recall his name, played a scale, allowing her to tune her instrument to his.

Harris tapped his stand twice, raised his hands, and the orchestra performers raised their instruments, ready to play. He counted off the opening with his hands, and the room came alive with the classical sounds of Dvořák.

Mina's hands shook with each note she played, and she felt like she couldn't remember how to move her bow correctly over the strings. She was used to playing under pressure, but there was something in the way the director kept glancing at her that threw her off. It was like Harris had changed into an entirely different person when he looked at her.

Lost in thought, everything else fell away. The musical tone of each note played, swirled around her like ribbons of various colors. The succulent notes made her mouth water, giving rise to a sweet, citrus taste.

A sharp minor note played, instead of a major, brought a sour, almost nauseating taste to the back of her tongue. Her bow hold felt odd, off even, and the usual pressure of the chin rest against her neck and jaw made her uneasy. Light, fluid strings waved in the air. A split second later, her stand partner gasped.

The horse hairs of her bow came loose, falling limp against her arm.

She didn't know if she should feel upset or embarrassed. How had she, an exceptional student, always on honor roll, who played the violin as if it were as important as breathing, been so shaken that she broke her favorite bow playing third violin?

The rest of the orchestra kept playing, and no one, other than her stand partner, had noticed what happened. Mina thanked the universe for that one small kindness.

She slid her instrument case out from underneath her

chair, extracted her extra bow, then returned her case to its resting spot under her seat.

"Are you okay?" The person next to Mina whispered, having stopped playing for a moment.

Mina nodded, and they lifted their violins back to their chins and then kept playing.

With her favorite bow now in ruins next to her chair, all Mina could do was follow along with the music and hope her old student bow would work. She listened to how the rest of the orchestra played together and taken by the lyrical chemistry this group had, many playing together for the first time. It's rare that she had ever heard an orchestra she was in playing at this level. Usually, she was right in the middle of the orchestra, but hearing it from the far-right side provided a novel experience entirely.

Mina kept her eyes down, staring at the sheet music and avoiding any kind of communication with the director. Resting both feet flat on the ground, she reveled in the subtle vibrations the music made on the floor. The cadence of the piece became her heartbeat, and the crescendo and decrescendo each breath. Fully immersed, she got lost in the sound, allowing herself to dissolve into the musical score. And for the first time today, she felt calm—a sense of inner peace.

4

Nico Fratelli

As Nico walked through Lewis Hall, he had to weave in between students who were just getting out of their first classes of the semester. A door opened suddenly, almost hitting him, and another stream of students flowed out into the hallway, adding to the congestion.

Hmm. Is this where Mina ran off to? He hung back against the wall, letting the traffic thin before he tried to continue on his way to Harris' office.

He peeked around the door and made way for the last of the students to exit.

"Who was that girl you sat next to, Toby?" A cellist, Javier if he remembered correctly, adjusted the shoulder straps of his instrument case. "The one who showed up late?"

"Oh, Mina? Yeah, her bow broke."

"That blow, man."

"Tell me about it. She had a cheap student model for a backup, so I let her borrow one of mine for her audition this afternoon."

"You know her?"

"I've seen her around. She's friends with Alyssa. Why?"

"She's kinda hot, right?"

"Sure, like in a weirdo way."

"What do ya think she'd say if I asked her out?"

"Man, I don't know. I've never seen her with anyone. She seems kinda reserved."

"Ha, bet she has a wild side. Might be a fun brief experiment. Take her out for a drive or two, you know? Show her the stars."

"Oh God, seriously, man." Toby shook his head. "Whatever you do, just remember, Alyssa's dating your roommate. So, she knows where you sleep, dude, and she's scarier than Satan."

"Ha. Probably worth it to see what Mina's like . . ."

They turned a corner, and Nico realized he'd been standing in place to listen to their conversation, even though the hallway was clear enough for him to continue on his way.

"Geez," muttered Nico to himself. "Am I a creep?" He pinched the bridge of his nose, wondering what had gotten him so worked up. It's not as if he knew Mina—really knew her. So, what did he care if those guys tried to mess with her?

It's not as if they're gonna get anywhere. Mina won't go for that. Will she?

He started walking again, hoping to pull himself together for his first day of TA work for Director Harris. Nico had heard the rumors about the man's style of leadership, and he didn't want to take any chances by making a bad first impression.

When he got to the door of Harris' office, it was halfway open. The man sat behind his desk, and a student stood in front of him, with her back facing the door.

Nico knocked on the doorframe to announce himself, hovering in the hallway, not wanting to interrupt.

Harris looked up at the sound of his knock. "Ah, you must be my new TA."

Nico nodded, unsure how much verbal conversation the man wanted.

"Well, I have your first task for you already. Can you take Miss Lu here to one of the practice rooms for her placement audition? I'll join you in a moment. There's a family matter that's come up, and I have to make a call."

"Sure, we'll wait for you there. I hope everything's okay with your family," said Nico.

Director Harris only grunted a reply and seemed to wait for Nico and the young woman to leave.

"Miss Lu, if you'll follow me, I'll get you all set up."

"Thanks." Her whisper barely audible.

When she turned around, his heart skipped a beat or two. It was Mina, Autumn's new roommate.

Mina walked out of the office to join Nico in the hallway, giving him a small smile before looking the other way. He felt oddly hesitant and wondered if she even remembered who he was. They had only seen each other briefly, and she had probably been more focused on meeting Autumn, and rushing to class, than looking at him.

Director Harris closed his door, leaving him alone in the hallway with Mina.

"Hey, Mina, right?" Nico asked, even though he was already sure it was her. "We met this morning. Well, I guess it was only like two hours ago." He tugged at the hem of his shirt, hoping it looked purposeful instead of just being a nervous habit.

"Oh, yeah." Mina seemed startled, as if she hadn't expected him to remember her name. "You're Nico? You're Autumn's—"

"Yep." The fact she remembered his name brought a smile to his lips. "Sorry, what where you saying? Didn't mean to interrupt."

"It's okay."

Nico and Mina walked a few steps in silence. He felt some pressure to continue a conversation.

"Uh, so, why didn't you just audition at the beginning of class?" Nico swore at himself internally.

Why would I say that? Now she thinks I don't want to see her.

"Oh. Sorry, this must be an inconvenience, I just couldn't—"

"No. No. You don't have to be sorry. It's—"

"—because I was late for class."

"Oh, God, I'm sorry, I interrupted you again." Nico tugged on the back of his hair to try to calm his nervous energy.

"It's okay."

"What did you say? I couldn't hear you over . . . uhm, the sound of me cutting you off."

Mina laughed, and Nico thought he saw her blush.

"I was late to class and missed the auditions this morning. Harris told me to stay after, and he'd take me to audition somewhere else."

"Why didn't you audition in the sound room?" Nico hoped he didn't sound annoyed with her again. That was the last thing he wanted her to think.

"Well, the storm from last night broke the air conditioning. Maintenance came around and fixed it during class, so the stage was cool, but the sound room was still hot.

"Oh, good to know."

"Harris said it would be better for me to concentrate if we went to a practice room instead. They'll be more comfortable since they're smaller and probably cooled down again."

"Can't argue with that, I guess." Nico could still feel some humidity in the building's air, but it seemed to be cool enough.

"I can't wait until this day is over." She sighed.

"Why is that?"

"Waking up to wet floors and missing the bus wasn't an

impressive start to my day. Plus, I broke my favorite bow this morning during practice. A classmate let me borrow his extra one, which is better than using the one I got in high school. Oh, and Director Harris said there'd be some extras bows in a closet by the practice rooms."

Nico laughed. "First the storm, late to class, and then your bow brakes? Is this a bad luck day, or is this normal for you?"

"No, definitely not normal. But at least it's not boring." Mina smiled and adjusted the strap of her bag on her shoulder. Nico realized she was carrying a lot and wondered if it would be weird if he asked if she needed help. But they were too close to the practice rooms for it to be useful, anyway.

Mina opened the door to the first room she passed and stepped aside. "After you," she said with a smirk.

Nico had never really been the most romantic person. He and Autumn had spent the last few Valentine's Days together, laughing at Hallmark movies and their cheesy, unrealistic depictions of relationships and love.

But Mina was different. Nico felt his heart beating a little faster when he looked at her, something that had never happened to him before.

He imagined telling Autumn about this, but he was afraid she'd turn it into a joke at his expense. Or worse, she'd tell Mina about how he felt.

That wouldn't go well. He sighed. *I don't even have a chance.*

5

Mina Beth Lu

Once inside the practice room, Mina's nerves somehow heightened. She was overly aware of how small the room was, and silently swore at herself for not having chosen one of the larger rooms further down the hall.

Even with the door opened, the room seemed strangely private—intimate even.

Mina busied herself by fussing around with the music stand, adjusting the height even after she had gotten it perfect.

Nico pulled a chair against the far wall, which was only a few feet away from where Mina stood.

She knelt on the floor and opened her violin case. "Oh, shoot, the bow." Mina stood up. "If it's not too much trouble, I'd, uhm . . ."

"I've got it." Nico sprung out of the chair and left the room.

Mina wondered if it was just an excuse to get away from her, and the uncomfortable silence between them. She spread out the papers Director Harris had given her on the music stand, then tried to decide which one she wanted to audition with.

The first two sheets looked pretty typical for audition sight reading. Not too technical, but still at an advanced level. The third sheet in the folder was different. Mina held it in front of her, surprised to find it handwritten. It looked like the original copy, too.

She ran her fingers over the notes, feeling the little indentations that the pen had made in the paper. At the top, there was a single note that read 'somber.' It comprised mostly long held notes, with a few sections of sixteenth runs, with a few grace notes here and there. It looked deceivingly simple to play, but Mina knew it was a piece that would rely on individual talent, giving a lot of room for expression and vibrato. It was a bit of a risky choice, especially since she only had a few minutes left to practice before the director came.

Nico walked back in the room with a bow. "Sorry, it was the best one I could find."

"Thank you, I'm sure it'll work." Mina took the bow from him, picked up her violin and put it to her chin. Uneasy, she set it down again and looked at Nico. "I'm just going to practice a bit."

"Oh, yeah. Of course. Do you want me to go outside?" He stood before Mina could reply.

"No, no. You can stay here. I just didn't want to play without . . . I don't know, announcing it?"

"Yeah, I get it. Do you want me to stay?"

"Yes," she said, surprising herself by replying right away. "Stay. I'd like that."

She lifted the violin to her chin again and went through a few scales, making sure that she was still in tune from class earlier.

Mina wondered why she was so nervous. She had done

countless auditions before, and while there were always some nerves, she hadn't felt this way since her first auditions when she was a freshman. Why did this one feel so much more important? She was already in the advanced class. It was just for a placement within her section.

In the back of her mind, she knew it was because Nico was in the room, listening—she was almost sure of it. But acknowledging that would mean also having to accept something about him made her nervous, which felt like too much of a betrayal to her new roommate.

She sighed quietly, wondering how much longer she was going to have to wait until she could stop thinking so much about her roommate's boyfriend.

As she continued to play scales, she quickly regained some of her usual confidence.

When she was playing violin, she felt like it was the only time she could be herself, unapologetically. Glancing at the hand-written score, she lost track of everything but the music, her violin, and her hands. The room seemed to fade around her as she played.

Even though she was looking at the music for the first time, the song came naturally to her, as if written specifically with her unique musical expression in mind. When she finished playing a few minutes later, Mina's own ability shocked her.

"Wow, Mina," said Nico. "I had no idea you were . . . man, you're really talented."

Mina smiled confidently. "Thanks." she reached for a pencil out of her bag, searching the music for a place she might need to make some notes, but couldn't find any significant part she had trouble with. Her mistakes were minor, just working out the kinks of playing something for the first time. Nothing that another play through wouldn't fix on its own.

"Do you have any notes or suggestions?" She glanced at Nico.

"Naw." He shook his head. "I don't think so. Sounds like you're ready."

She looked at the door, checking to see if Harris was coming, and a new wave of nerves bubbled in her stomach.

"I'm sure you'll blown him away." Nico's smile brightened his piercing blue eye.

6

Nico Fratelli

Not that he hadn't thought Mina would be a capable musician. He knew she was in the most advanced music class the school offered, but he had never heard of her before helping Autumn move in.

Nico had been an active member in the music department for four years, having known exactly what he wanted to major in when he started his freshman year. He had assumed he knew all the best musicians in the department, at least by name. But he was confident he had never heard of Mina Beth Lu.

How was it possible that someone who played so beautifully, could go unnoticed as a department favorite?

Nico was almost sure he had never seen her before, either. He would have noticed her immediately. She was exactly his type. Long black hair with little bangs, a willowy figure, prone to side-eyes and smirks. Autumn's clothes, a big and understated, hung on Mina, but Nico imagined she would wear something more expressive—feminine.

He tried to think about anything other than Mina, and what she would wear, but his mind remained stuck on one thought—Mina.

"Are you a transfer student?" He stood in the open doorway.

"No." She inspected the bow, then pulled out some rosin. "May I?"

"Yes. Of course."

The exquisite sound of her violin echoed around in his head long after she had stopped playing. Nico struggled to find something else to say that would fill the silence between them. Even though he wanted more time alone with Mina, he couldn't help but look to the door to check if Harris was close. He thought that maybe if he had more time to think before he talked to her next, he might impress her with a discussion on a rare composure. He'd have homework for sure.

Harris walked into the room. "Sorry about that. The call took longer than expected." He rubbed his hands together. "So, are you ready, Miss Lu?"

"Yes." She nodded. "Uh, is everything okay?"

"Oh, yes, I think it's all going to work out just fine." Harris gave Mina a wide smile.

He turned his head slightly and looked surprised to see Nico leaning against the wall.

"Oh, Nico, you can go wait in my office. When done here, I'll come meet with you about your coursework for the rest of the semester."

Nico nodded. "Of course, I'll see you then." He was disappointed about leaving because he wanted to hear Mina play again.

7

Mina Beth Lu

When Harris walked into the practice room, Mina was a little relieved. Making small talk with Nico was difficult, and she felt like she was just stumbling over her words.

It's probably for the best, Mina thought. *I shouldn't be spending so much time with him. I don't want to make things weird with Autumn.*

But when Harris asked Nico to leave, Mina felt a sliver of disappointed. He had liked the way she had played, and she couldn't help but want to play for him again. It was one of the few times she felt confident in herself, and the music had filled up what might have otherwise been empty silence between them.

"So, did you look over the music?" Harris asked.

"Yeah, I got to play through one of them. I can pick which one I play, right?"

"Of course." Harris sat down in the same chair Nico had used and pulled over a spare music stand to use as a desk, so he could take notes on Mina's performance. "Which of the two did you pick?"

"Which of the two?" Mina asked, confused. "There were three different songs in the folder you gave me. I uhm, I picked the last one. The handwritten one." Mina's stomach dropped, nervous that she had done something wrong.

"Handwritten? Can I see it?"

"Yes, Sir." Mina passed the sheet to Harris.

"Oh, it seems you've found one of my personal pieces."

"You wrote that?" It surprised Mina. "The piece is beautiful."

"This is the one you practiced?"

Mina nodded.

"Well, I guess it wouldn't hurt for you to use it for your placement audition. But you better get it right. After all, you're playing in front of the composer."

Mina could tell that Harris was joking, but it made her feel even more nervous than before.

Harris sat back and crossed his arms. "Well, whenever you're ready, Miss Lu."

Mina took a deep breath to center herself, then she picked up her violin. Her thoughts emptied with the first pull of her bow across the strings. The sound, deep and succulent, echoed around the practice room.

Her fingers moved across the neck of her violin as if she had already learned the song by heart.

When Mina finished playing, the last note reverberated around the small room.

"Bravo." Director Harris clapped a few times.

Mina's face turned red, and she looked away from his intense stare.

"Wow, that was incredible. I haven't had the chance to hear that song played by someone else yet, so thank you for that."

"Y-you're welcome," stuttered Mina.

8

Nico Fratelli

As he started walking down the hall toward the director's office, he heard Mina play through some scales, signaling the first part of her placement audition had begun. He couldn't help but linger to listen to her play. Harris wouldn't even be back in his office until the completion of Mina's audition, so he had time to listen to her play that song again before heading off.

Other students had filled up the empty practice rooms along the hall, and Nico saw someone who looked like the guy he had heard talking about Mina earlier. He was meandering down the hall toward Mina's practice room, and where Nico was standing.

Nico resisted the urge to say something to him. Partly because he didn't want to make a scene, and he didn't know what he would realistically say.

Phrases tumbled in his head. *Stop talking about Mina? You better not talk to Mina? She would never go for you. You're not her type.*

Nico realized he didn't know much about Mina. He had no right to interfere in her life, even if it was to defend or protect her. So, he looked away, waiting for the guy to pass, or go into a practice room. But he didn't. He just kept walking, slower and slower. It was then he realized Toby was also listening to Mina play. Eventually, the guy sped up his walk, keeping a regular pace.

When he passed, he nodded to Nico and said, "Whoever that is, they're great."

Nico didn't reply, annoyed that he had talked to him at all. After he had turned the corner, and Nico was alone in the hallway again, he felt strange.

Am I really any better than that guy? Nico thought. He was listening to Mina play, and he had been thinking about the way she looked, just like that other guy.

Nico shook the thought out of his head. There was a difference between a genuine interest in someone and whatever crude notions that guy had about her.

Still, he couldn't quite shake the memory of the conversation he had overheard. He tried to rationalize how angry he had felt, by sticking to the assumption, the guy was unprofessional, not to mention held little to no respect for woman.

In the practice room, Mina played the last few measures of the song.

"Bravo." Harris clapped.

Nico hurried out of the hallway and toward Harris' office, worried about what he would say if he caught Nico eavesdropping.

9

Mina Beth Lu

Harris made some scribbles onto a paper that Mina couldn't see. He flipped through a few other papers that were below it.

Mina fidgeted, unsure of whether she could put her violin down yet.

"We'll, you might not be the most popular in class, but I'm going to move you to first chair."

"F-first chair?" Mina's heart raced, both with excitement and fear. "Wasn't someone else assigned first chair today?"

"Yes, we did auditions and some preliminary assignments today, but I clarified that all arrangements are malleable for the first week. Keeps everyone on their toes and practicing every day."

"Thank you, Mr. Harris, this is an incredible opportunity." Mina set her violin carefully in its case.

"Please, call me Oliver. And guarantee, with a talent that great, you'll have many, many more opportunities in your future." Director Harris stood and moved to shake Mina's hand. "Actually, I have a proposition for you."

"What is it?" Mina clipped her violin case shut, then took his hand.

"That piece you played, it's part of a chamber piece I put together. I recruited a small, talented group of select students to perform it. But the violinist had to drop out at the last minute. Does this sound like something you'd be interested in? The performance is next week, so you'll only have a few days to get your part down. You'll get credit hours for it, of course."

"Wow, yes, thank you. That sounds incredible." It stunned Mina. She had never gotten recognition like this in the department before, despite having been a student for two full years. She had always suspected it was because she was quieter than a lot of other music majors, afraid to take risks with her auditions and extracurriculars.

Graduating in three years, also meant she had less time than most other students to make a name for herself, and she had worried she wouldn't be able to graduate with any notoriety to her name. But the opportunity to be both first chair, and in a professor's pet project orchestra, was more than she could have dreamt of. It would be a hard week learning the music, but she had played that one part so naturally, she was confident she'd be able to pull it together in time.

"I'll need that copy back. It's an original. But why don't you stop by my office tomorrow afternoon, and we'll talk more." Harris took the folder and extra music from Mina's stand and slipped the notes he had taken during her audition into the folder.

"I will. And Director Harris, thank you."

"Okay then. Practices are at six every night until the performance on Saturday. Have a pleasant afternoon, Miss Lu." Harris walked out of the practice room and started on his way to his office.

Mina stood still in the practice room for a few minutes after he left, wondering if it had all been a dream.

Her phone rang, and she jumped a bit as her phone made a small sound. When she checked it, she saw that it had been a notification from her calendar. "Oh, shoot," she muttered, realizing she only had ten minutes to get from Lewis Hall to her job at the call center on the other side of town.

She grabbed her violin and her bag, walking as fast as she could to the front door of the building. She didn't have time to go back to her room and drop off her violin. Depending on the bus schedule, it would take her about thirty minutes just to get to her room and back outside again, so she would have to take the violin with her. It would be a hassle, but it would be safe under her desk while she worked.

Once she made it outside, she called a taxi and rushed off to the call center.

Nico Fratelli

"Hey, Kid, eyes up," Uncle Henry's voice boomed. "Look lively, now."

Nico snapped to attention. "Sorry, Uncle Henry."

"And no leaning on the wall." His aunt walked into the storefront from the back room. "You're still too young to be slouching, Dear." Her arms were full of new duet books for the new display he just finished building.

"Yes, Aunt Eden." Laughter slipped between his lips.

Standing up straight, he busied himself. He cleaned the register area, swept the dust off the computer, straightened out the display of guitar picks at the counter—twice, and then pushed the receipts down in the trash bin with his foot.

Mondays were usually slow, so the shop closed earlier than usual. There was only an hour left until five, and Nico watched the bell over the door, praying that it wouldn't ring.

His aunt and uncle kicked no one out of the shop after closing time. Nico hated having to stay at the register and pretend not to watch the customers as they drifted around the store lazily. He had plans with Autumn after he got off, which was incentive enough to be eager for closing time, but he knew that seeing Autumn equated to another encounter with Mina.

"Boo." Uncle Henry goosed Nico's sides.

And just like when he was a little boy, Nico squealed then jumped.

"Gotcha." Uncle Henry patted Nico's shoulder "What are you thinking about so deeply, Son?"

Nico's face turned red. "It's nothing. School." His gaze slipped down to his shoes.

"I can tell something's on your mind. Ever since you were little, you've had that thinking face. Ya get your eyebrows all scrunched up, and you look at your shoes."

"I do not." His head snapped back up.

"Well, I can't force ya to talk to me. But I can force you to do your job. And if whatever's on your mind affects your performance, then we've gotta dilemma."

"It's really not a big deal, it's just been a long day."

"I bet it's a girl," chimed in Nico's aunt.

She stood in from the other side of the shop. For a moment, Nico wondered how his aunt could be so sharp, and thought he must have let some small detail slip earlier.

"When are you going to marry that girl, Nico?"

"What?" Confusion flooded his mind.

"You two are like peas in a pod," said his aunt. "Have been since Kindergarten."

"Oh." His face warmed with embarrassment again. "You mean, Autumn?" Nico shook his head. "You know it's not like that with her."

"Well then, who are ya gonna marry? You're running out of time, Nephew."

"I'm twenty-three, Aunt Eden. I haven't even graduated college yet."

"Ah, don't listen to her, Nico. She doesn't know what she's

talking about. We met when we were well into our thirties, didn't get married until we were almost forty."

Nico nodded, thankful for his uncle's verbal save. It seemed like he had heard this story a hundred times since his aunt and uncle took him in as a toddler. And today, he was more than happy to hear it again if it meant changing the current subject.

He knew that his aunt was coming from a good place, wanting him to find someone to settle down with. The last time any of them had heard from Nico's mother was on his tenth birthday, a simple, "Missing you," scrawled onto the back of a postcard like an afterthought. As Nico got older, he doubted she even remembered it was his birthday, and the timing of the card was just a coincidence.

His aunt always worried about him inheriting the "wild" gene from his mom and uncle's side of the family. No matter how many times he assured her that he wouldn't pick up one night and leave them, she wouldn't stop worrying about it.

Other times, she'd pull Nico into a tight hug with her hand on the top of his head as if he were a little kid, even when he grew a full foot taller than her. She'd state something like, *'I'm grateful for that 'wild' gene, or else we wouldn't have gotten you.'*

"Well, if you will not tell us what's up with you, at least go help your poor old aunt carry those books."

Nico jumped at the chance to get out from behind the register. "Here, let me get those." He took the books out of his aunt's hands.

"Thank you, Sweet Boy." She patted his cheeks, pinching one gently.

Nico had always thought of his aunt and uncle like his actual parents, and hardly ever felt like he was missing out on anything by not knowing his biological mother and father.

Nico felt guilty, not confiding in them about what he had

really been thinking about. As he watched his aunt bring out more books from the back and his uncle count up the day's earnings at the cash register, he decided it wouldn't do any harm to tell them about his day.

"Fine, I'll tell you. But you have to promise you won't make a big deal out of this, okay?"

His aunt and uncle stopped working and looked up at him.

"I mean that." He looked from his aunt, to his uncle, then back to her. "Please, don't make this into something that it's not."

"Oh, of course we won't." His uncle had that all-knowing glint in his eye.

The same glint that reassured Nico, his uncle would, in fact, be the first person to make it a bigger deal than it needed to be. He thought for a moment about changing his mind, but he could tell that they were excited, and he didn't have the heart to back out.

"When I was helping Autumn move in this morning, I met her new roommate, who seems really nice. I haven't gotten a lot of chances to talk to her, but I might see her later tonight, when I'm with Autumn."

"What's she like?" His aunt put down a few books on the edge of the counter.

"Well, I'm not really sure. We talked for a few minutes, but I don't know. We were both kind of shy. But she plays violin so beautifully, Aunt Eden, you would love her."

"What's her name? Bring her around here sometime. Maybe on a date?"

"Her name's Mina, and if I asked her on a date, I would definitely not bring her here."

"I don't see what's so wrong about bringing a date home to see us." Nico's aunt huffed.

"Aunt Eden, if I ask her out, you will be the first person to know, I promise."

"And you'll bring her to meet me?" His aunt's eyes sparkled.

"Of course. If I ask her out, I will eventually bring her here to meet you, and Uncle Henry. I promise."

Nico's aunt smiled. She grabbed the books, then pushed them into place on a nearby shelf. "Well, none of us are getting any younger."

Mina Beth Lu

The call center was always a strange mixture of silence and conversation. To Mina it almost felt like a library, but everyone was on the phone. Most of her coworkers didn't talk to each other. And they all spent most of their shifts on the phone, so they didn't have much time to socialize, anyway.

Walking down the narrow pathway between desks, she was careful to be as quiet as possible, so she didn't disturb any calls. Rounding the corner, she stepped into her cubical.

Mina settled in at her tiny desk, carefully sliding her violin case onto the floor under her chair.

A sliver of the window above the small walls surrounding her desk offered a glimpse outside. It surprised her to find the sky growing dark. She hadn't noticed another storm rolling in, but then, she had mostly focused on getting to work on time, and not what the weather was like. She had brought an umbrella with her just in case, so she would be fine if it was still raining by the time she went home.

She had only just settled in when she got her first call. Mina took a deep breath before answering the phone. She tried to shake off the eventful day, so she could focus on her job.

The first few callers she got were pleasant enough, and she didn't have to handle any yelling or insults being hurled in her direction. Callers were nice. She answered calls for a pet clothing company, and the person who buys into this business is usually kind.

A few hours into work, Mina took a brief break at her desk. Her audition after class had left her ill-prepared for work, so she didn't have a book for mind-food like usual. So, she scrolled through social media on her phone, and her heart picked up speed when she saw Nico had added her on two different platforms.

Is this weird? Mina accepted, and followed back, telling herself it was completely normal for someone you just met to follow you on things. Plenty of people she'd never met at all followed her, so Nico's requests shouldn't be any different.

Mina still felt strange, though. She didn't have Autumn on anything, and she her roommate. So, she figured she should add Autumn too. It's the friendly thing to do. Plus, it'd show Autumn she wasn't trying to get close to her boyfriend.

It was only halfway through her shift, but Mina had already started counting down the minutes until she could leave. The sky was growing dark, and she contemplated whether she was going to order another car to get home. They were pricey, and if she paid for a ride both too and from work, it would eat up half of what she earned that day.

Mina decided that it would be worth the risk to walk home. There would still be some light out, and it was only about two miles. Usually, she would have taken her bike to and from work, but since she didn't have that her options remained limited.

The fluorescent lights in the office flicker overhead.

"What the hell was that?" Asked someone a few desks away, say.

In a flash, all the power to the building turned off.

A small amount of light filtered into the room through the windows, but it threw most of the office into a heavy shadow. Murmurs spread through the room as everyone was trying to figure out what was going on.

A long rumble of thunder sounded, followed by a quick flash of lightning in the distance.

Mina's boss, Harold Bass, showed up at the front of the room.

"Okay, everyone," yelled Harold above the noise. "Looks like there's a storm coming in. Power's out for this side of the town and won't be back for a while. Work crews are working to get the power lines back up. But since it's only an hour before the day ends, you're free to head home before the storm hits."

Everyone immediately started gathering their things and filing out of the office. Mina let most of the crowd dissipate before she started leaving, so that her violin case wouldn't get in anyone's way.

Out on the street, Mina saw a few dark spots on the sidewalk where early raindrops had fallen. She felt nothing coming down yet but saw a few flashes of lightning in the distance. Her dorm was in the opposite direction the storm was moving, so she thought she would make it home before the rain started. She scurried fast, just to be safe.

The street was quieter than usual, and dusk made the shadows of the buildings ten times their proper height. Mina felt the hair on the back of her neck rise but tried her best to ignore it, blaming her uneasiness on the fact that the street lamps hadn't come on yet. She was safe here, had never run into any trouble before.

She was only a block away from work when a boom of

thunder hit. Grabbing her earbud, she streamed some music over her phone.

Something large and heavy hit her shoulder with bruit strength, shoving her onto the sidewalk.

A yelp escaped her lip.

Her forehead hit the rough sidewalk, and a small amount of blood drip down her face.

Before she could recover from the impact, someone ripped her backpack off her shoulders, then wrenched her arms together, yanking her up and off the sidewalk a few inches. A man wrestled the strap of her purse from her hands, and she tumbled to the ground.

"Fire," screamed Mina, remembering that much from the basic self-defense course she had taken during high school gym class. "Fire. Fire."

The man wearing a beany who had attacked her, ran down the street and disappeared into an alley with her purse. She sat up, trying to pick out any identifiable features she could recall, but the shadows were too dark, and swallowed him before Mina could fully process what had happened.

She heard more footsteps running in her direction, and she jumped up and turned around, expecting another attacker. Mina recognized the person approaching as someone who worked in her office, but she couldn't recall her name.

"Are you okay?" The woman panted as she ran the last few feet.

Mina burst into tears and looked around. He had taken her bag and her violin. She had some minor scrapes and bleeding down her arms and on her forehead, but nothing broken other than her heart and resolve over the loss of her instrument.

"Oh, sweetie. What happened?"

"He took my stuff." Mina told her through teary hiccups about the mugging. "My violin."

The woman rested a hand on Mina's shoulder reassuringly. "Did you call the police?"

Mina shook her head. "My phone was in my purse." A fresh wave of tears unleashed.

"It's okay, I'm calling now." She put an arm around Mina's shoulder.

Nico Fratelli

A vintage horror slasher scene played out on the laptop at the foot of the bed, and a bag of microwave popcorn sat between Nico and Autumn.

Knock.

Knock.

Knock.

Nico jumped and bumped heads with Autumn.

"You heard that, right?" Autumn slid down, pulling the covers to her chin.

"Yeah, someone's at the door." Nico reached out to pause the movie.

"Should I—we open it?"

"I'll get it. It's probably nothing." Nico stood and walked to the door.

Why he every let her talk him into watching a knife-wielding psychopath on his laptop tonight was beyond him. He approached the door with caution, then reached out and grabbed the handle.

Knock.

Knock.

Knock.

The sound boomed just as a clash of thunder struck, and he jumped.

"Who is it?" Autumn's voice was barely audible.

"Shh." He hushed her with a finger to his lips. "I'm about to find out."

He opened the door a crack, then flung it open. "Mina?"

Nico stood still, shocked. She had blood dripping down her face from a cut on her forehead, and there were scrapes and dark, angry bruises up and down her arms.

"What happened?" Nico quickly stepped aside and let the still-shaking Mina into the room.

"Oh, my God, Mina. Are you okay?" Autumn jumped off the bed and ran toward her.

Nico wanted to do something, anything, but he didn't know what to do for her.

"Do you want some water?" He held her teary gaze.

"No, thank you." She shook her head, then turned to Autumn. "I got mugged. They took everything."

Mina fought another round of tears but couldn't hold them any longer.

"Hey, it's gonna be okay," said Autumn. "Let's get you cleaned up." She guided her into the middle of the room.

"Oh, Autumn, your clothes. I'm so sorry."

"Don't be. I have plenty of other clothes. Let's just worry about you, all right?"

Mina nodded, tears falling onto her cheeks.

Nico longed to holder, to comfort her, but again, he didn't know what to do.

"Stay with her, Nico." Autumn ran to the bathroom and grabbed some paper towels and a wet washcloth.

Nico cleared some of Autumn's clothes off a chair and pulled it out, so Mina could sit down. He took her gently by the shoulder, wrapped an arm around her, then led her through the room.

She trembled against him. It pained him to see her like this.

Once Mina was sitting, Nico squatted next to the chair, so he could be at eye level with her. "Can you talk about what happened?"

Mina nodded slowly. "I was walking home from work." She sniffled. "The guy came out of nowhere." Raising an arm, she wiped the tears from her eyes with the back of her hand. "I shouldn't have been wearing headphones, I know that, but I really didn't think—"

"It's not your fault." Nico took her hand in his.

Mina shrugged, unconvinced.

Autumn came back into the room with some towels. "Do you need help to clean up?"

"No," said Mina. "Just—do you have any band aids?

"There should be a dorm first aid kit in the hallway closet." Autumn left the room again to get the supplies.

"Are you okay?" Nico took one of the damp paper towels and helped her clean the dried and oozing blood off her elbow. "Sorry. I know I keep asking that. Is there anything you need? What can I do?"

"It's okay." Mina smiled. "Thank you. You've done so much already."

"Have you called the police yet? You should tell them what happened."

Autumn walked back into the room and handed Mina some disinfectant and bandages for her cuts, then leaned against her bed.

"Yes." Mina nodded. "A co-worker of mine called the police. They wrote up the report and gave me this." She pulled a police incident report card out of her front pocket.

"What did the police say?" Nico put some antibiotic

cream on a bandage, then taped it to her arm, covering her elbow. "What are they gonna do?"

"Nothing." Tears dribbled down her cheeks, but her tears were slowing. "I didn't see his face, so there's no information they can use to try to find him."

"Well, if you had your instrument insured—"

Mina cut him off. "I didn't."

"You should also file a report with the school. There might be other robberies that happened around the area. Someone else might have given a description." Nico shrugged. "You never know what might be helpful."

"I guess you're right," said Mina.

Nico nodded at Autumn, who reached for her phone to dial campus police.

"I don't know what I'm going to do now." Tears started leaking down Mina's face again. "I don't have an instrument. How am I going to graduate?"

Nico took her hand in his and gave her a reassuring squeeze. "It'll be okay, we can figure that all out later. For now, you can talk to the campus police." He rose. "I'll get you a nice dinner, and then you can rest, okay?"

Mina nodded. "I'm sorry, guys."

Nico could tell she was feeling guilty he and Autumn had to do so much for her. They'd only just met her this morning, but it all seemed like it was so long ago.

Mina pulled her hand away from Nico's, and he tried not to feel disappointed.

She rubbed the last few tears from her eyes and looked up at Nico. "I don't know how to thank you for this."

"You don't have to," said Nico. "I'm just glad I can be here to help."

Autumn put down her phone. "Campus police said they'll pull your police case report, and that you should go in tomorrow if you want to make a report with them, too. But there's nothing they can do right now."

"Thanks, Autumn. Thank you both for your help." Mina stood up, still shaky. "I'm probably just going to go to bed." She walked to her suitcase.

"Hey, isn't that stuff still damp?" Autumn rummaged through one of her plastic bins. "Here, you can wear these." She handed Mina a T-shirt and sweats."

"I don't want to—"

"I insist," said Autumn with a firm voice.

He could tell exhaustion weighted Mina's eyelids, and he watched her stagger into the bathroom to change. Once the door clicked closed, Nico turned to Autumn.

"I think I'm going to head out," he said. "I ordered some pizza for you two, so I'm gonna go pick it up."

"Okay." Autumn nodded. "Hey, Nico."

"Yeah?"

"Thank you," said Autumn. "I don't know what I would've done if you weren't here."

"What are you talking about?" Nico asked, confused. "You helped just as much as I did."

"Yeah, but I probably wouldn't have held her hand."

Autumn smiled, and Nico turned his head away, embarrassed.

"I'll make sure she's okay. Let me know when you're on your way back with the food."

"Will do." Nico left, shutting the door slowly behind him so it didn't make any sudden noises.

When he got outside, he let out a deep breath. It had really rained while he was inside.

Black worms squiggled in puddles strewed across the sidewalk in front of the building. He looked down as he walked, making sure he didn't step on any of the squishy worms.

13

Mina Beth Lu

When Mina woke the next morning, Autumn was still asleep. So, she shut off her alarm quickly, worried it would wake her roommate. She knew Autumn would try to convince her not to go to class, but Mina was afraid of missing out, especially since she had just gotten placed as the first chair. Mina figured that if she showed up a few minutes early and had time to talk to Harris before class started, they might figure out some way that Mina could continue to play. The college had a few extra bows, so they might also have a few extra violins—maybe one she could borrow until she found a more permanent solution.

Regardless, Mina didn't want to wait any longer than she had to. She looked into the small makeup mirror that sat on her desk and messed with her hair, trying to see if she could brush it out in a way that it would hide the cut on her forehead. It was healing but looked even worse than it had the night before. Some extra bruises had formed since the last time Mina had looked in the mirror, and there was no way she could hide those with another bandage.

Autumn muttered something in her sleep, then turned over. Mina paused, staying quiet, so she didn't wake Autumn.

Mina checked the time on her phone and picked up her pace. So, used to running late, she didn't really know how to plan on being early. Each measurement of time in her head, she calculated carefully, so she knew what the absolute last minute she could leave her room was, and still be able to get to class a few seconds before anything started. It was as if being early was like learning an entirely new system. Mina had to keep recalculating how many minutes it would take her to get to class, just making sure she had thought out all the math correctly.

As she left her dorm, she felt oddly naked without the weight of her instrument in her hand. Everything else seemed to go the way she wanted, though, and she was thankful for that measure of success. But she owed this sliver of cheer to waking up after the first alarm went off, and because of the fact she was out the door a minute before she needed and caught the bus on time. It seemed like only a matter of seconds before Mina was standing outside Lewis Hall.

She slipped in through the tall, heavy doors of the building and walked down the hallway toward her classroom.

When Mina got there, she saw that the room was empty. Mina paused, unsure of what to do next. She hadn't expected that Harris wouldn't already be there, but it was ten minutes before class started.

Mina shut the door and turned around to face the hallway.

The footsteps and murmurs as other students filtered to her ears. Other people walking through one of the many halls, slowly making their way to their next classes.

A thought came to her. *Perhaps Harris is in his office getting ready to today's instruction. Or he might have already been on his way.* Either way, Mina decided it would be best to just walk toward his office. She would catch him one way or another, and still have a few minutes to talk before everyone else arrived, or so she hoped.

She started down the hallway, navigating the way to the director's office. Mina shoved her hands in the pockets of her skirt, nervous about having to talk to Harris.

What if he kicks me out of the class? Or worse, doesn't believe me when I tell him what happened last night? Mina thought.

In the back of her mind, she knew that with how much her talent had impressed Harris, there was no way he would just let her stop playing. Plus, he needed her for the concert he was putting on in a week, and likely wouldn't be able to get anyone else to join at the last minute like Mina had.

The hallways were still mostly empty, despite there being less than ten minutes before the next classes started. Mina was overly aware of how sharp the sound of her footsteps were, echoing around the linoleum floors and wood-paneled walls. She hurried along toward Harris' office, wanting to get it over with as quickly as she could.

When she got to his door, Mina took a deep breath before she knocked softly. She could tell the light was on inside but didn't hear a reply. After waiting for a few moments, she knocked louder.

"Come in," Harris called through the door.

Mina slowly cracked the door open and hovered in the doorway. Harris was sitting at his desk, typing something on his computer.

"Oh, Mina," said Harris casually, looking up from his computer. "How are you?"

"Well, actually, that's kind of why I'm here."

"Is something wrong?" Harris rested his elbows on his desk, suddenly serious.

Mina didn't know how to answer him. She didn't want to talk about how she was feeling because she worried, she would start crying again if she told the entire story, like she had the night before with Nico and Autumn.

"Last night"—she swallowed hard—"when I was coming home from work at a call center in town, I . . ." Mina looked down. Her eyes burned and tears welled, threatening to overflow. She hoped Harris wouldn't notice. "I got mugged. My violin was with me." Mina tried to look as casual as possible. She even turned away long enough to wipe a stray tear off her cheek. "He took everything."

Harris didn't utter a word. The heavy air that fell between them offered a deafening silence that sucked what little resolve she had left.

Mina couldn't tell if he was just thinking, or if he was waiting for her to say something else.

Anxious, Mina tried to fill the silence. "I just came to tell you, uhm, I won't be able to play today and might need some time to figure out how to get a new violin. I'm really sorry if this messes with your plans."

"Mina, it's not your fault," said Harris. "Are you okay? Did he hurt you?"

"I'm fine. Only a few cuts and bruises. Nothing that won't heal in time."

"Glad to hear that." He held her watery gaze. "Look, I think I can find you a violin to play."

"Really?" Mina didn't trust her ears. She was hesitant to have hope until she was holding another violin in her hands.

"Yes, really." Harris smiled at her. "I have one that I think you'll love."

"T-thank you." She had never expected to see a resolution this fast or easily and had just assumed it would take at least a few days to figure something out.

"I can have it for you to play today. It's lucky that I had it with me today."

"Wow, yes. Thank you so much." Mina felt excited. She knew she would probably have to return the violin at the end of the semester, but she felt like she was getting a gift.

"Go on to class, and I'll meet you there in a few minutes with the violin." Harris nodded at her, which Mina took as a cue to exit.

She took a step out the door, barely able to contain her excitement.

"Actually, Mina, if you could wait a moment."

"Yes?" Mina paused at the door. Her enthusiasm turned to dread.

Oh, no. Has he changed his mind? The thought made her eyes water all over again.

"You said that this happened after work, when you were walking home, yes?"

Mina nodded, unable to find her voice.

"What would you say if I offered you a job here, in the music department? I've been looking for a student to be my assistant this year."

"I would love to." Mina paused, trying to curb a fresh wave of excitement on the emotional rollercoaster she rode as an unwilling participant. "But isn't Nico your TA?" She didn't want to step on anyone's toes.

"Yes, Nico is my TA. But as my assistant, you would have more advanced work. I need someone to assist with changes to a few new scores I'm working on, help me take notes, and possibly do some scheduling for future performances?"

"That would be incredible. When would I start?"

"How does tomorrow sound?"

Mina was so excited, she felt almost like she was floating. "Yes, Sir. Tomorrow sounds wonderful."

"Great. Hang around after class ends today, and we can

talk more about specifics." Harris gave Mina another small nod, and she turned back toward the hallway.

As she walked out, Mina turned around again and glanced at Harris. "Thank you!"

14

Nico Fratelli

The front stairs of Lewis Hall were one of Nico's favorite places on campus. It was on the side of campus that housed the older buildings that had been around since the college was first founded. Chipped brick sidewalks lined the path. The bird nests, tucked safely beneath the roof's overhang, contained life each spring. And a large willow tree hung its branches over a small pond, providing shade to the aquatic inhabitants.

He sat there and listened to the sounds of footsteps, passing cars, and bird songs. He was usually the only one there in the early afternoon, which suited him just fine.

"Hey." Mina came up behind him.

Nico jumped, part of his coffee splashing out of his cup and onto the steps.

"Oh, shoot," said Mina. "I'm so sorry!"

Nico laughed. "It's fine. I just wasn't expecting you is all." Nico paused. He hadn't seen Mina for a few days since the night she got mugged. He had missed her, but worried that if he told her, it would scare her off. Or worse, she'd laugh in his face. "Haven't seen you in a while where've you been?"

"Oh, you know. Around." Mina laughed. "Mostly, I've been living in the practice rooms."

This surprised Nico, and he wondered why Mina would need to practice so hard this early in the semester. "Wow, you're pretty hardcore then."

"No, not really. It's not for the performance at the end of the semester." Mina shifted the weight of her bag to her other shoulder. "I'm working in Harris' chamber orchestra, playing music he composed. The concert is on Saturday."

"Wow, congrats! I've heard about that. It's very exclusive. He only ever asks the best of the department to play."

"Well, thanks, but I only got it because their original violinist had to back out at the last minute. So, I've been practicing this whole week to make up for the lost time."

Nico could tell by the way Mina kept shifting her feet, he was keeping her from going somewhere. He grabbed the handle of his bag and stood up, not wanting to take up too much of her time.

"I was just about to go see Autumn." Nico lifted one strap of his bag onto his shoulder.

"I'm going back that way too. Wanna walk together?" She gave him a shy, sideways glance.

"Yeah, I'd like that." Nico hoped he didn't sound too eager.

He walked at a leisurely slow pace down the tree-lined path and wondered if it was strange how his footsteps changed pace to match Mina's, or the way his hands hung at his sides. All he could think about was what it would feel like if he reached out and held Mina's hand in his.

On their way back to the dorms, Nico got to know Mina better. Her favorite color was purple. She started playing violin when she was seven. She liked raisins in cookies and mushrooms on pizza.

"Hey, can I ask you a favor?" Mina turned to look at Nico.

"Sure, what is it?"

"Uhm, Harris invited me to this dinner tonight. A little music department thing at his house to celebrate the concert tomorrow." Mina paused.

Nico thought she looked nervous.

"Would you want to go with me? I'm just . . ." She swallowed hard. "I'm kind of afraid to go alone at night, you know?"

Nico felt his heart race. *Is this a date?*

He reflected on her words and tried to stifle the goofy grin that tugged at his lips. A department gathering wasn't exactly romantic, but he didn't care. It would give him a chance to spend time with her, and that's all he cared about. Plus, it made him feel good to know she trusted him enough to ask him to accompany her to the party.

"Yeah, that sounds cool." He tried to keep himself from feeling disappointed that it might not be a date. He was glad Mina thought of him to invite at all.

"Sorry. I know this is such a brief notice. But I was going to run over after stopping at my room to change."

"That's okay? Am I good to go like this?" Nico was wearing jeans and a plain t-shirt, which wasn't what he would typically wear to this kind of event, but he knew he wouldn't have time to go back to his room and change.

"Honestly, I don't know." She chewed on her lower lip. "But I'm not really going to dress up, so I'm sure you'll be fine." Mina smiled.

After they got on the bus, they didn't talk much. The crowded interior of the bus forced Nico and Mina to stand so close, her arm pressed against his. Mina was quiet, and looked away from him, but didn't try to stand further away.

When they got outside Mina's building, Nico said, "I'll just wait outside."

"You don't want to come in and see Autumn?" Mina fished around in her bag for her keys.

"Nah, it's okay. I texted her that my plans had changed." Nico couldn't decipher the expression that Mina looked at him with. It was something like confusion, but not exactly. He brushed it off, telling himself that it was just his nerves making him overthink.

Mina went inside to change, and Nico sat on the front steps of the building. While waiting for Mina to return, his phone buzzed with a text from Autumn. It said: are you going on a date?

Nico's heart raced. He wondered what Mina had told Autumn. He wrote back: I'm not sure, what do you know?

Autumn wrote: nothing she's just taking a long time to pick a dress.

Nico wondered if she was nervous to be going out with him, or if the nerves resulted from going to a professor's house. He figured it was a safer bet to keep assuming that it wasn't a date, because it would be less embarrassing than to have incorrectly thought it was something more.

But when Mina walked out of the building in a flowy black dress with shimmery silver stars, Nico couldn't help but stare. He noticed how the dress fit her perfectly, as if made just for her.

Mina smiled. "Ready?"

Nico nodded in response, afraid that if he said anything, he would just make a fool of himself.

It was only a ten-minute walk from the dorm to Harris' house. It surprised Nico how easily his conversations with her flowed in that short amount of time. Mina seemed to gain some confidence with each step, and he liked the way she stole brief glances at him when she didn't think he would notice.

Harris' house was large and imposing, one of the few remaining original houses from the 1800s—from the founding of the town. The steps creaked as Nico and Mina made their way up.

He paused, waiting, wondering if he should knock for both of them, and if since he was the guest, if he should wait for her to knock.

Mina took in a quick breath, stepped forward, then knocked on the door.

Harris opened the door with a smile stretching from ear to ear. A look he didn't think he'd ever seen before. "Hello, Mina. I'm glad you could make it."

"Me too. Thanks for inviting me—us."

When Harris saw Nico, it seemed as if disappointed cast a shadow over the man's face.

Nico's palms itched, and they got sweaty.

Am I not supposed to be here?

"Come in." Director Harris' voice seemed clipped, annoyed even. "Follow me."

Nico motioned for Mina to go first, then he followed her through the door. Harris immediately led Mina through the entryway and into the room where people had gathered. It was a light crowd, but as Nico tried to follow them, they seemed to slip away in the sea of people.

"Hey, Nico," called out one of the other professors, Mr. Leon, in the department.

Nico smiled, and obligingly went over to talk to him for a moment, even though what he really wanted to do was track down where Mina and Harris had gone.

Now and then, he saw a few glimpses of her silvery dress through the growing crowd. But each time he thought he would catch up to her, another group of professors or music department TAs and students pulled him into another conversation.

He believed he saw her talking to someone, but it wasn't Harris.

By the time Nico could excuse himself, it looked like

Mina and the unfamiliar man she was talking to were deep in a conversation. Nico didn't want to intrude, but when he caught Mina's eye, she looked distressed.

Nico walked closer, trying to figure out what was going on.

"Wow," the man grinned, looking over Mina as if undressing her. "You're even more beautiful than I imagined you'd be."

"Thanks," replied Mina with an uncomfortable laugh. She crossed her arms over her body and looked back at Nico as if asking for help.

Nico walked up behind Mina and rested his hand on her shoulder. "Hey." He tried his best to sound casual, but he looked at the man talking to Mina with disdain. "Sorry to interrupt, but Mina, there's someone I want you to meet over there."

Mina didn't hesitate. In fact, she looped her arm through Nico's, letting him lead her away.

Nico leaned close to her ear, then asked, "Who was that?"

"Harris' son," grimaced Mina. "Actually, I'm not feeling so good. Do you mind if we just head out?"

"Yeah, of course we can." Mina kept her arm through Nico's.

Each time he and Mina encountered a crowd, she tightened her grip. He navigated the path, backtracking the way he came, and before long, he slipped out of the house with Mina, with no one noticing.

As they walked home, Mina didn't mention the man she was talking to, Harris' son. Nico wondered if there was something he should say, or if it would be too intrusive if he asked what they had been talking about. He could tell Mina was uncomfortable and tried to cheer her up instead of making her think about whatever Harris' son had said.

When they got outside of Mina's dorm building, she paused at the steps.

"Hey," said Nico. "This was fun. I mean, despite being a bit of a disaster."

Mina laughed. "Well, it got me out of the practice rooms at least."

Nico shifted his feet nervously, trying to think of what to say next. He wondered if he could ask Mina on an actual date, but wasn't sure if she would even want that, especially after what happened at Harris' house.

"Hey." Nico grabbed the door and opened it for her. "If you ever need another excuse to get out of the practice rooms, I'd be happy to help."

"Thanks." Mina paused. "I might take you up on that sometime."

Nico smiled, attempting to look casual while he internally calculated the cost and benefit of being blunt with Mina, and asking her out.

Mina took a step inside. "Well, goodnight."

"Night." Nico watched to make sure she got into the elevator safely, and then turned and walked away, cursing himself for missing the opportunity to ask her out.

15

Mina Beth Lu

As she walked out onto the small stage and sat down, Mina felt the gaze of a full audience on her. She adjusted her stand nervously, fighting the urge to move it so it blocked her face from the audience. The hardest part of performing wasn't the music, it was the knowledge you were being watched.

Mina knew that one of those people in the audience would be Harris' son, Dustin. But she also knew Nico would be there, and his presence offered a calming reassurance. The nerves he caused in her, the flutter of her stomach, seemed superficial compared to how uncomfortable she felt around Dustin.

When the rest of the musicians had settled down at their seats, Harris lifted his arms, signaling all performers to raise their instruments and to get ready to play. He tapped off the tempo, brought the baton down, then it started playing.

Mina focused on the music, trying to make herself forget about everything but the notes in front of her. With the bright lights shining on the stage, she couldn't see out into the crowd at all. As they got further into the first song, Mina let herself blend into the sounds of her violin. She pretended it was an extension of herself until she really believed it, and the only thing in her mind was the next few measures that she had to play.

The rest of the concert went by in a blur. Mina effortlessly hit all the notes, never making even the smallest mistake. Music was what she knew best, and no matter what was happening in her life, she could always come back to her violin and feel a balance in the world again.

After the last song, the orchestra stood, and the audience clapped. The musicians filed off the stage in an orderly line. Without the music, Mina's thoughts creeped in again. She knew she would have to talk to Dustin again—it was unavoidable.

Before the performance, Harris seemed so intent on having them talk.

Did he know about the advances Dustin had made?

Mina wondered if there was a way, she could talk to Harris about it, but she didn't know what she would say. She didn't feel comfortable telling him that his son was making her uncomfortable.

What if he took it personally and fire me? She sighed.

Deep down, she knew she needed to keep working with Harris. He was her professor, after all, and she couldn't drop his course and still graduate on time. Plus, she couldn't risk losing the violin he let her borrow, knowing that she could never buy herself another one.

She loved the opportunities that Harris was giving her. It was basically her dream job, doing some original composing and having someone as accomplished as Harris to help her. This work was setting her up for the future that she wanted and was an opportunity that she probably wouldn't get again.

As Mina walked out of the backstage door and into the crowd of audience members that was growing in the hallway, she felt like she was going to be sick. She scanned the crowd nervously, looking for Dustin.

Instead, she locked eyes with Nico. He gave her a warm, reassuring smile, and Mina wondered if he knew why she was so nervous. She smiled back, and he started walking through the crowd to where she was standing.

"Mina," he said, once in ear range. "Your performance was amazing."

Mina blushed. "Oh, thank you."

"I can't believe you learned all of that in a week," said Nico. "It really seemed like you had been practicing just as long as everyone else."

"Well, I spent almost all of my free time catching up."

Nico fidgeted with his hands, and Mina wondered if he was nervous or if he just had nothing else to say. For a few moments, Mina wondered if she should say something that would make Nico feel like he could leave if he wanted to, but he broke the silence before she could figure out what to say.

"If you need something to do with your new free time . . . we could go get coffee or something?"

Mina froze. *Is he asking me out?* She knew that she had to say something soon but wasn't sure how Autumn would take the two of them getting coffee without her.

"Yeah, that could be fun," said Mina, hoping that she sounded neutral. When I get home tonight, I'll invite Autumn. Mina knew that by inviting Autumn, she would know that Mina wasn't hiding anything.

Nico's brows furrowed in confusion. "That's nice of you, but you don't have to invite me because—"

"Mina," shouted Harris over the crowd. "You did such an amazing job." He angled his body in such a way that he gave Nico his back, but still faced her.

Mina wondered if he did that on purpose, like he was trying to cut Nico out of the conversation.

"Oh, thank you. You did a magnificent job, too. That music is beautiful."

"The department set up a little celebratory dessert table in the common room. You should stop by. The rest of the orchestra will be there, and my son, Dustin."

Harris looked at Mina, but she hesitated to answer.

"I'd like to talk to you about starting some work you'll be doing as my assistant, too."

Mina knew that there wasn't a way she could refuse after he brought up the assistant work. "Of course, I'll head over in a few minutes."

Mina looked past Harris to Nico, who looked uncomfortable, and Mina was afraid he was about to leave.

Glancing over his shoulder as if to see what Mina was looking, Harris seemed surprised to find Nico standing there.

"Ah, Nico. I didn't notice you there. You're welcome to come too, of course." Something in Harris' tone told Mina that he didn't really mean it. But she looked at Nico and widened her eyes, trying to tell him she needed him to come.

Nico smiled awkwardly. "Yeah, sure, that sounds fun."

Mina could have sworn she saw Harris' mouth twitch into a frown for a split second before he smiled. "Great. I'll see you both there." Harris walked off toward Dustin and a few other members of the orchestra.

Once Harris was out of earshot, Mina said, "Thanks, Nico."

"Yeah, of course." Nico moved a little closer to Mina and whispered, "It's Dustin, right?"

Mina nodded. "I just don't know what he wants from me. And I don't really want to deal with that alone. I'm sorry to drag you into all of this."

"It's okay, really." Nico smiled. "I promise."

Mina took a deep breath and let it out slowly. "All right, let's get this over with."

16

Nico Fratelli

The school facilities department set the common room up with a few tables and chairs. A small dessert buffet on the far wall had cookies, finger cakes, and glasses of punch.

Nico led Mina over to the table, hoping that it would distract her, and take her mind off of whatever troubled her.

"Hey look, this one has raisins." Nico grabbed one of the raisin cookies and handed it to Mina.

"I can't believe you remembered that." Mina laughed. She broke off the edge of the cookie and ate it.

"How is it?" Nico asked.

"Not bad." Mina smiled. She looked over his shoulder and her smile faded.

"Harris or Dustin?" Nico asked.

"Dustin." Mina rolled her eyes, but Nico could tell that she was more nervous than she let on.

"Hey Mina." Dustin walked over, completely ignoring Nico. "I've been looking around for you."

"I just got here," Mina said with a shrug.

"Cool." Dustin glanced over at Nico and then looked back at Mina, without ever acknowledging Nico's existence.

Nico had never met Dustin before, but immediately had about ten reasons he could rattle off on why he hated him already.

One, Nico thought, *he makes Mina uncomfortable.*

"I was wondering if I could talk to you about something." Dustin held Mina's gaze.

Two: *Dustin is one of those people who skates through life with just a small amount of charisma and a bland appearance.* He sighed.

Mina looked over at Nico before replying to Dustin, and Nico gave her a quick smile, trying to convey that he would be there for her if anything went wrong.

"Sure," said Mina. "But I don't have too much time, I have plans later."

"Great." Dustin surprised both Mina and Nico by taking Mina by the arm and leading her away, so they could talk in private.

Three: *the guy's a control freak.*

Nico stayed back but made sure he was still within hearing distance of them. He worried about Mina but didn't want to control her or make her feel more uncomfortable than she already was. He figured she had enough of that between Harris and Dustin.

The night Mina came back to her room after the mugging came to mind. He trusted her to make smart choices, but he worried there would be another situation that she couldn't control by herself.

Dustin muttered something to Mina, who kept taking subtle steps away from him, even as he tried to get closer. It seemed like he was showing her something, but Nico couldn't see what it was.

When Mina took a noticeable step back, Dustin grabbed her arm forcefully and pulled her closer.

Nico raced forward. "Look at the time." He clasped his hand over Dustin's, prying him loose.

Mina, shaken, ambled out of reach.

The glint of something metallic in Dustin's hand caught Nico's eye, but before he could get a good glimpse, his fist closed around it, and Dustin put whatever it was back into his jacket pocket.

There were a few people in the room that had noticed the commotion, but it was crowded enough that they hadn't caused a scene.

"Remember, you have that thing. You don't want to be late." Nico wrapped an arm around Mina's shoulders, protectively blocking her off from Dustin.

Dustin's jaw jutted out, and the muscles of his face tensed. "We are talking here and don't need—"

Four: the guy's not only controlling, he's a controlling asshat.

"Thanks for the chat, but we're leaving now." Nico walked Mina out of the common room, her frame trembled against him.

He thought about how much he wished he could have said something cooler—even cursed himself for not doing so. Once they were out in the hallway, Nico guided her to a bench.

"What happened," he asked softly, "are you okay?"

"Yeah, I'm good. It was just weird." Mina sat and nervously tugged on the ends of her hair. "He tried to give me a ring,"

Nico took a seat next to her, his knee touching hers.

"A what?" He shook his head, not sure he heard her right.

"An engagement ring. He was saying something about how he couldn't let someone like me just walk away."

She didn't pull away from him, so Nico relaxed a bit.

Five: he's more delusional than the Mad Hatter on opioids, psilocybin mushrooms, and LSD.

"That's insane," said Nico. "Do you think Harris knew he

71

was planning this? It seemed like he really wanted the two of you to meet."

"I don't know." Mina sighed and leaned against the wall. "Yeah. Maybe. I think Harris might have planned this. Is that crazy? Am I making this into something that it's not?"

"No, you're not crazy." Nico leaned on the wall next to Mina. "It sounds like you're right."

"I don't know what to do." Mina's voice shook. "Dustin said that Harris told him I'd be easy to win over. And that I was in their debt because of the violin he gave me. That and the job as his assistant."

Nico fought the urge to reach out and hold her, knowing that might make her feel even more uncomfortable. "You aren't really considering this, are you?"

"I don't know. Everything's closing in. What with the mugging, the concert, and now this?" Mina looked at the floor. "But if I don't, I'll lose everything." Her eyes watered.

Nico sat in silence, unsure of what to say to her. He didn't even know how long she'd known Dustin.

Maybe they have history.

"Dustin's not that bad. Maybe I can reason with him." She cradled her head in her hands. "I don't want to lose everything I have going for me right now. I've worked too hard." She looked back up at Nico, making eye contact. "I think I have to do this."

"Please, Mina, just take some time and think about it," Nico begged.

Mina nodded and wiped a stray tear off her cheek with her sleeve.

"I need to get my purse out of my locker. Will you go with me?"

Nico nodded, then escorted Mina back into the common room. Harris was walked out of his office. Nico figured he was planning on confronting Mina but didn't expect to see him there as well.

Harris put on a big, friendly smile. "Hi Nico, mind if I borrow Mina for a second? I'd like to talk to her in my office about her assistant work."

"Actually, we were—" Nico didn't want to leave Mina alone with Harris.

"It's okay, Nico. It'll just be a minute." Mina gave Nico a reassuring nod, but Nico could tell she was nervous.

Nico wander around the common room, knowing that leaving was the wrong decision. With each step he took, he felt even more anxious about what Harris was saying to Mina. He feared that Harris would abandon her in a room with Dustin, who could hurt her, but that was unlikely —wasn't it?

Back in the common room, Nico looked around, unsure of what to do. He didn't know many people there, and besides, he didn't think he could hold a regular conversation, given the situation. Nico looked back at the door and realized it was opened just a crack. He could see Harris and Mina. If he stood close enough to the door, would be able to hear them.

Nico made a loop around the room, so that Harris wouldn't be able to see him walking back up to the door. Once he got all the way around the room, he leaned carefully against the wall next to the door. There, he could hear their conversation, but they could not see him. Praying that Dustin wouldn't arrive, or that no one would come try to talk to him, Nico did his best to look casual. He took out his phone and pretended to be texting, covering the fact he was trying to eavesdrop on Harris and Mina.

Through the murmurs of conversation drifting around the common room, Nico could only hear parts of their hushed conversation. He could tell Harris was angry, and probably would have been yelling if it wasn't so important that they didn't attract any attention.

"Do you know how lucky you are?" Harris said. "With my

help, you could have everything you've dreamed of. All you have to do is accept my son's proposal."

Mina muttered something that Nico couldn't hear.

"You don't have to get married right away." Harris sounded exasperated, as if Mina was the one saying something absurd. "Just accept the ring, and you can take some time to get to know him. You can keep the violin, it'll be yours. Do you know how much it's worth?"

"N-no," Mina stuttered.

"Sixty thousand dollars. You'll never get a violin like that again. And your job as my assistant? I don't think I can continue to work with someone who has disrespected my family."

"Please," she said.

Nico could hear tears in Mina's voice.

"I'll lose my scholarship if I didn't have an instrument. I won't be able to graduate."

"That's not my concern."

There were a few seconds of silence, and Nico wondered if they had left. Just before Nico was going to check on them, Harris spoke again.

"There's no need to cry," he sounded warm and sympathetic, but there was something about the way he said it.

Nico felt a small chill run down his spine at the sudden shift of tone.

How could he change so quickly? Nico wondered.

Harris continued to speak, and his tone lost some of its warmth. "Just take a week to think about things. I'm sure if you got to know Dustin, you would feel differently about his proposal. Until you make your decision, let's postpone your assistantship with me. And I'll hold onto the instrument."

Nico heard Mina's voice but couldn't make out her reply.

"Get back to us by next Friday. And Mina, think about what's best for your future."

The sound of Harris' lumbering footsteps faded down the

hallway, and Mina shuffled slowly back into the room. Her eyes widened in surprise when she saw Nico just around the corner from the door.

"How much did you hear?" She asked.

"All the important parts," replied Nico. "Do you want to talk about it?"

Mina nodded. "Can you, uhm, walk me home? I don't really want to talk about it in public."

"Yeah, that makes sense. Come on, let's get out of here."

As they turned to walk out of the building, Nico reached out his hand to Mina instinctively. When he realized what he was doing, it was too late to pretend he wasn't reaching for her hand. For a second, Nico was so afraid of what Mina's reaction would be, it felt like his stomach was turning into stone.

After those few painful moments, Mina reached out hesitantly, and Nico wrapped his hand around hers. They walked out of the building like that, holding onto each other.

17

Mina Beth Lu

Mina couldn't help but feel guilty as she walked into her room in tears for the second time that week.

"What happened?" Autumn sprang out of bed. "Did the guy come back? Did you see him?"

"No, but it'd be better than this."

"What? I'm lost." She grabbed a soft drink off the computer table. "Somebody better start talkin' and fast."

"It's a long story." Nico sat down at Autumn's desk.

"I got time. Well . . ." Autumn glanced at the time on her phone. ". . . until my class in twelve hours and fourteen minutes. So, what gives?"

Mina leaned against her bed and took a deep breath, trying to get rid of her tears. She worried about how Autumn would react to how close she was becoming with Nico, but at the same time, she tried to tell herself that wasn't something she should put her energy into at the moment.

"Do you promise not to tell anyone?" Mina asked Autumn. "I don't want anyone to get in trouble over this."

"Yeah, sure." Autumn nodded, confused. She jumped back up onto her bed, and sat on the edge, leaning forward.

Mina started the story of what had happened with Harris and Dustin. She tried to keep it short, so she didn't take up too much of Autumn's time, but in the end, it took her almost an hour to get through the whole, bizarre situation.

Autumn did her best not to interrupt, which Mina found helpful. But a few times, her roommate broke in to say things like, "What a creep," and, "I'll fight him."

Mina had never appreciated Autumn more than she did in those moments.

Autumn was supportive while, at the same time, made Mina laugh, despite how upset she was.

Mina finished telling her story. "And that's everything."

Autumn asked, "So, what now?"

Mina tapped her fingers against her bed frame. "I'm not really sure."

"He's just trying to manipulate you, Mina," said Nico. "It seems like he's been planning this for a while."

The room was silent for a minute. The three of them tossed out different possibilities the director had really arranged this elaborate scheme to manipulate Mina. It seemed impossible, but all the evidence was there.

"It just seems so surreal." Mina rubbed her eyes and face.

"Why else would Harris have given you a sixty-thousand-dollar violin?"

"Director Harris didn't give it to me. He's letting me borrow it."

"Sure, he is." Autumn slurped her drink. "And he's also giving you an assistantship opportunity, a spot in a prestigious orchestra, setting you up for concerts, and putting you in the first chair seat all out of the goodness of his heart. Yep. It's official. He's a jackass."

"Even if he did this all on purpose, it wouldn't change anything." Mina sighed, sinking down to sit on the floor.

Autumn looked at Nico, as if unsure of what to do. She jumped down off her bed and sat on the floor next to Mina, and Nico followed. The three of them formed a little triangle. Just having the two of them close made Mina feel supported.

"You don't have to do anything you don't want to," Autumn murmured in a calming tone.

Mina teared up again. "I know, b-but I can't stop thinking about everything that I'll lose if I say no. I'll have to drop out. What am I going to do without graduating? Everything I've done in my life has been to prepare myself for college." Mina tugged at her hair.

"Wait." Nico stilled her hand movement. "What would you need, if you said no to Harris?"

"What do you mean?" Mina asked.

"Like, what would you need, theoretically, in order to stay in school?"

"A lot. Too much. I would need another violin, or else I can't take any classes, and I'd also lose a portion of my scholarship and the work study pay. So, I'd need a job, too. And I can't go back to the call center, after I quit so suddenly. Why didn't I think things through?"

"Don't worry, we got your back." Nico reached into his pocket and took out his phone. "What would you say if I told you that I could help you? With everything."

"Are you serious?" Mina was hesitant. She wanted to trust Nico, but his confidence was so sudden, she didn't know how she should react.

Autumn gasped. "Oh, right. Yes. How did I not think of that?"

"What is it? What's going on?" Mina looked back and forth from Nico to Autumn, who both just grinned at her.

"My aunt and uncle own a music shop." Nico unlocked his phone, and soon Mina heard his phone ringing.

"Nico?" a warbly voice came from the phone's speaker. "What is it? Is something wrong?"

Nico put his phone on the floor between the three of them. "No, nothing's wrong. Don't worry, Aunt Eden. I just need a small favor."

"A favor?" His aunt's melodious voice oozed through the phone.

"Yeah. I have this friend . . ." Nico paused and looked at Mina. "She's in a bit of a situation.

"A favor?"

"Yeah, can you put Uncle Harold on too?"

"I'm here, Boy. Now, what's this about a favor?"

"Well, you see, my friend, Mina, she got mugged and lost her violin. Even had to quit her job because of it."

"Is this the pretty girl you were telling your uncle and I about?"

Nico flinched and reflexively moved to take the phone off speaker mode just in case his aunt said anything else embarrassing.

Autumn laughed and pushed his hand away from the phone with a smack.

Mina's face turned red, and she busied herself by pinching at the carpet.

"Yeah, that's the one," said Autumn, still laughing.

"Well, I was thinking," Nico cut in. "Maybe you could use some extra help around the shop? And in return, Mina could borrow one of the violins in the back?"

"Well, I'm sure we can figure something out," his aunt said warmly. "Why don't you bring her by tomorrow, so I can meet her?"

Nico looked at Mina and raised his eyebrows. She nodded her head and smiled to confirm that she could go.

"Yeah, I'll come by with her after you close the shop," said Nico.

"Or you could come by and help us close up, both of you."

Uncle Harold's voice boomed through the phone. His smile evident.

Nico grinned. "Okay, we'll come by to help you close. I've gotta go now, but I'll see you tomorrow. Love you guys."

"And we love you too, dear," she responded, and then Nico hung up the phone.

"Is this real?" Mina asked, in complete shock.

"It's real, I promise," said Nico.

Mina leaned over and hugged him, and then Autumn. "You have both been so much more helpful than I could have ever asked for. Thank you."

"Of course." Autumn hugging Mina back. "Friends help friends, no questions asked."

18

Nico Fratelli

The day went by slower than Nico thought could be possible. He counted down the hours until he would see Mina later that day. The store closed at six, so he planned to pick Mina up from her dorm at five, so they could walk over together.

It was almost five, and Nico couldn't stop checking the time on his phone.

When he got a text from Mina saying she was getting ready to go, his heart leapt. He knew this wasn't even close to a date, but he was just excited to get to spend some more time with her, outside of a stressful situation. It seemed like every time they were alone together. It was because something terrible was happening.

A few minutes before five, Nico headed out to meet Mina. He walked at a brisk pace, hoping to calm himself down before seeing Mina. But with each step, his anticipation only grew, and by the time he was outside her building, his heart was racing.

Mina was waiting for him on the steps and waved.

"Thank you so much for doing this." She stood and walked over to Nico.

"You know, you don't have to keep thanking me." Nico laughed.

"I know, but I don't know how else I can repay you for everything you've done for me."

"You don't have to repay me at all. I'm just happy to have the excuse to spend more time with you." Nico contemplated again about whether he should just tell Mina how he felt. When she smiled at him, he thought she might feel the same way. But whenever he got close to asking her out, she seemed to become withdrawn.

He didn't want to risk making her uncomfortable, especially since they were going to be working together now. It might just make her feel like it was a repeat of what happened with Harris and Dustin, and he didn't ever want to cause her to feel that upset.

As they walked to the shop, they chatted casually. Nico was happy to have time to talk to Mina about regular things, like how their days were going, and how excited they both were for the beginning of fall.

"The equinox is only a few weeks away." Mina gave him one of those sideways glances he found endearing.

"The what?" Nico asked.

"The equinox." Mina looked at Nico playfully. "It's the first day of fall. It's when the day is the same amount of time as the night."

"Equal light and dark," said Nico.

Mina nodded. "I like keeping track of time like that. I don't know, it just helps me feel more stable when the seasons change."

"I can understand that." Nico recalled how often the changing seasons seemed to go by so quickly. Sometimes it could feel disorienting, and he would wonder how all that time had passed in what only felt like a few days.

As they walked down Main Street, Nico watched Mina's reflection cross the shop windows. He liked the way her hands swayed gently, how the hem of her skirt bounced with each step she took. He even liked the way the wind blew her long hair into her face.

Mina reached back and held some long strands of hair in her hand to keep it out of her eyes. She looked to the side and caught Nico's gaze in the glass.

Nico quickly looked away.

"How long have you been working for your aunt and uncle?" Mina asked.

"Pretty much ever since I can remember. They took me in when I was just a baby. My mom had run off somewhere. She was always traveling. It wasn't a suitable lifestyle to have a kid around. So, my aunt and uncle are more like my parents."

"Oh, I'm sorry."

"No, it's okay. I'm honestly glad she went away, or else I wouldn't have had the amazing childhood I had with my aunt and uncle. And I wouldn't be where I am right now." Nico looked over at Mina, who avoided making eye contact with him.

"Your aunt and uncle sound like phenomenal people. I'm excited to meet them."

"Well, that's really lucky, because we're here." Nico pointed to the music shop's door, which was only a few feet ahead of them.

Nico held the door open for her and then followed her into the shop.

"Harold," his aunt called out. "The kids are here."

"Remember what you said earlier, Aunt." Nico kissed her on the cheek.

He had called his aunt and uncle earlier in the day, begging them to be normal around Mina and to not mention anything that he had said about her in the past. He also gave them a small overview of the situation, so they could understand why it was so important that Mina could get a job there.

"Why, look at you." His aunt greeted Mina with a big smile and an even larger hug. "You're prettier than a little ladybug, yes you are."

Mina laughed and hugged his aunt back. "Uhm, thank you."

"What's all the commotion?" Uncle Harold pushed through the stockroom door. "Now, why didn't you tell me the kids were here?"

"I was keepin' them all to myself." She winked at Mina. "He's a little deaf on the right side, dear."

His aunt took Mina by the hand and started showing her things around the shop and making small talk.

Nico knew this was mostly just a way to get to know Mina better but was glad his aunt was at least trying to mix the rapid-firing of questions with telling Mina about the store and the job.

"Why don't we start with showing you how to take inventory at closing?" His aunt led Mina into the back of the store.

Nico went over to the register and busied himself with starting to tally the total earnings of the day. He tried to focus on his task but couldn't help worrying about what his aunt might talk to Mina about.

When Nico finished counting the earnings, he checked the clock. There were only five minutes until the shop closed, so he slowly dusted off shelves and straightened instruments that were hanging on the walls, making his way across the shop toward the door.

When those last five minutes were up, Nico walked over to lock the door. Before he could touch the door handle, someone burst into the shop. At first, Nico assumed it must just be a customer coming in late. Annoyance hit him for a moment, knowing his aunt and uncle would never kick a customer out of the shop if they were there past closing. But when the person pushed his way further into the store, Nico recognized him.

"Dustin?" Nico asked. "What are you doing here?"

Dustin looked around the shop. Everyone but Nico had been in the back-storage room, teaching Mina how to do inventory. "Where's Mina?"

"She's not here." Nico lied.

"I know you're here, Mina. Come out," yelled Dustin yelled.

Mina slowly cracked the door and walked into the front of the shop, followed by Uncle Harold.

Nico hoped his aunt would stay in the back. He didn't want her or her uncle hurt in case things went wrong with Dustin.

"How did you find me?" Mina asked, shocked.

When Dustin didn't answer, she asked, "Have you been following me?"

"You've been ignoring my calls," said Dustin. "I had to see you. We need to talk."

"She need not talk to you if she doesn't want to," Uncle Harold cut in.

Nico walked toward Dustin, trying to make himself look stronger and more menacing than he was. "I think it would be best if you left."

Dustin looked around, assessing his options.

Nico knew that it was unlikely Dustin would cause a scene or pick a fight, but at this point, he didn't want to rule anything out.

Back to his mental list of reasons he didn't like Dustin, another one came to mind.

Six: he's a psychopath on a mission and focused onto Mina—my Mina.

"Fine," Dustin spat. He looked at Mina and pointed. "You don't know what you're throwing away. I promise, you'll regret this."

Nico followed Dustin closely through the shop, then slammed and locked the door after he left.

"Are you okay?" Nico approached Mina. Visibly shaken, she trembled.

"Yeah," whispered Mina. "Just a little surprised, is all."

"Ladybug." His aunt patted Mina's hand. "How long have you known that man?"

"Today was the third time I've seen him." Her eyes water a bit.

"Oh, let's not have none of that. Don't let him ruin your day. Now, you dry those tears." His aunt wrapped her arms around Mina, drawing her into a warm, maternal hug. "You're safe. And Nico here, he's gonna take good care of you. We all will."

"Thank you," sniffled Mina.

"It's okay if you want to go home for the day," said Harold.

"No, no," Mina shook her head, dried her tears, then a small smile touched her lips and brightened her eyes. "I'll be fine. Let's get back to work."

19

Mina Beth Lu

During her midmorning shift, she took on the task of taking inventory in the back by herself. Uncle Harold, keeping himself busy building shelves, making himself available, and had made light conversation with her. Well, it started off casual, with questions about what her major was, and where she was from. But after a bit, he talked about Nico.

First, he had said, "He's such a kind boy with a gentle heart."

Mina was a little confused why he was telling her this, but then she decided it was cute how much Harold clearly loved Nico.

The man kept talking, saying more about how great Nico was, until he finally made his point clear.

"You know . . ."—he stopped tinkering with the shelves—"he talks about you a lot, you know. But he's afraid how you would react if he asked you out on a date."

"What?" His words caught her off-guard. "But isn't he, uhm, dating Autumn?"

Harold laughed so hard, he had to rest a hand on the workbench to support himself. "No, he's not dating Autumn. They've been best friends since preschool."

Suddenly, Mina's confusion cleared. She was right about thinking Nico had feelings for her and considered what this would mean for her and him. All she wanted was to go out with him, but with everything else that was happening with Director Harris and Dustin, it was more complicated than ever.

And now, knowing Nico and Autumn were only friends, Mina thought about the plans she and Nico had made to get coffee.

Hmm. Did Nico mean it to be a date, she sighed, wishing she knew for sure. Or did he even want to go out with her? *What if he's only being nice?*

Her thoughts twirl around, replaying bits and pieces of the last few weeks.

Why did Dustin walk into the store?

Preoccupied all last night, thinking about the proposal, and what Dustin had meant when he said she was going to regret her choice, made for a sleepless evening.

Did I give off mixed signals, making him think I was interested when I wasn't? The same mixed feeling that had plagued her the last several hours, turned her stomach sour. *He probably meant I'd regret everything that I was giving up by refusing his proposal.*

But still, there was a strange, menacing tone to his words that went beyond the things she would give up. She couldn't shake off the feeling of fear all last night and didn't have the energy really to think about what Nico's uncle had said.

Even though Dustin's threat was still on her mind, Mina was just a few minutes away from the end of her shift, and from getting coffee with Nico and couldn't put off her nervous energy about him any longer.

"Is it okay if I finish the rest of the inventory tomorrow? I only have the paper goods left." She glanced over at where Harold was stocking a self with instrument cleaners. "Or, if it's okay, I could come back and finish the rest later this after."

"A split shift." Harold seemed to give this some thought. "Yes. That's fine. How about you finish up later this afternoon—you can catch a ride back with Nico, and he can show you how to close out the register."

"Thanks." She counted the Armstrong flutes, then marked down the number of each model on the form. "Plus, extra cash always comes in handy." A smile bloomed on her lips.

"Then I'll see you later." Harold gave her a nod. "You kids have fun."

She hung the inventory clipboard up, and by the time she had gathered her things, a cab waited for her outside, compliments of Harold and his wife. Making a mental note of their kindness, she decided to treat everyone to donuts and coffee during her next shift.

In the cab, she sat back, finally alone with her thoughts. It had been a few days since her first shift in the music shop, when Dustin had followed her. And ever since that day, she couldn't stop looking over her shoulder everywhere she walked, worried she would find *him* right behind her. Even though she had blocked his number, she still received texts from other numbers, begging her to talk to Dustin. And when she didn't reply, vague threats about what would happen to her if she turned him down, blew up her phone.

It was late afternoon by the time the cab pulled up outside her door. The common room, a large open space for students to mingle, was full of different groups of people—some studying and others playing cards or talking.

Autumn's laughter rung from somewhere in the room. She knew she should say hello, but with her coffee date rapidly approaching, she didn't want to risk being late. So, without stopping, she dashed by common area.

Minutes later, she stood in front of the mirror, trying to decide what to wear. The dress with ruffles was too poofy, the denim overalls were 'farmer girl' for the occasion, and the short and blazer her mother recently sent her wasn't warm enough yet.

So, she wondered why she felt so nervous about picking out an outfit to just get coffee with Nico, amid everything else. It was a different kind of nervousness, though, a good one.

As she sorted through her clothes, she over thought about what to wear. She didn't want to look like she was trying too hard to impress him, but she wanted to pick out something nice.

Finally, she settled on her favorite black dress with a little lace hem. It was a bit fancy for going to coffee, but as she was walking out the door, she pulled on her denim jacket and a pair of worn-out boots to dress it down.

Mina rushed out the door, worried she would be late. As she hurried down the sidewalk, she pushed Dustin, Harris, and even the mugging out of her headed. She only thought about Nico, and what she would say to him?

Should I apologize? Should I tell him I thought he was with Autumn?

A vehicle slowed behind her on the long stretch of the alley road. Mina glanced back just in time to see the side door slide open. A masked man jumped out.

Mina screamed and ran, but he caught up to her in only a few strides. He grabbed her, and put his hand over her mouth, muting her cries for help before she could draw any attention.

In just a few seconds, she found herself tied up in the back of the van, which was speeding off.

20

Nico Fratelli

She's only five minutes late. It means nothing, or so Nico told himself.

He was sitting alone at a table for two in the coffee shop. He felt the baristas watching him, wondering if he was just going to sit there or if he was going to buy something. Nico had wanted to wait for Mina to get there before he ordered. It would make it easier for him to pay for her if he just bought them both at the same time.

The longer he sat there alone, the more anxious he got. After ten minutes went by, he texted her to ask if she was still coming. After fifteen minutes, he wondered if he should leave.

Does she not want to see me? Nico pushed the thought from his mind.

Mina had seemed excited when they made the plans, and she had acted fine around him just the night before.

After twenty minutes went by and Mina didn't show or text back, he wondered if something bad might have happened. He hadn't thought Dustin or Harris would hurt Mina, but with the odd behavior, calls, and messages, he wouldn't put anything past them now—well, more so, Dustin.

Nico considered what his options were. He knew she had a split shift today, and the second part of her shift started in a few hours, so he headed over there to wait to see if she showed up. If he saw her come to her shift, he would have his answer, and know she just didn't feel the same way about him as he did about her.

But if she didn't show up, it would mean she could be in danger.

Nico got up and walked to the counter. "Two regulars with cream and sugar, one vanilla espresso, and one caramel special. Oh, and a carry box."

Vanilla anything is her favorite—especially when it comes to drinks.

He figured the least he could do was take a few coffees to his aunt and uncle. When the barista finished, he grabbed the box of drinks, then started the walk to the music shop.

"Nico," his aunt called to him the moment he walked through the door. A surprised expression shot her thin-shaped brows up. "What are you doing here so early? Thought you were grabbing coffee with Mina before work." She looked behind him, as if looking for someone.

He walked through the door. "She never showed up."

"Is she okay?" Worry clouded her gaze.

"I don't know." He shrugged his shoulders. "She seemed fine when I walked her home last night, and she texted me this morning to confirm what time we were going to meet. But she hasn't responded to my last few texts, when I asked if she was still coming." Nico walked to the register where he set the coffees. "I thought I'd wait to see if she makes her shift."

He eyes the vanilla espresso still in the carton carrier next to his uncle's.

"Do you think that man who came in here last night could have done something to her?" His aunt walked to the register and leaned on it with an elbow.

"No. Maybe." Nico, frowning. "I don't know."

Uncle Harold walked into the room. "Why are you here so early, Nico? Couldn't wait to see us?" He laughed at his joke. But when he realized the somber tone of the room, his face grew serious. "What's going on?"

"Mina didn't show up." His aunt sighed. "She's missing."

"We don't know that for sure." Nico shook his head. "Maybe she just doesn't want to see me."

"Oh, Nico." Aunt Eden patted his back. "I don't think that's the case."

"Well, I'd rather have her just not want to see me then have her be in some kind of trouble." Nico grabbed his coffee.

"Let's just wait here for an hour or so, until her shift starts." Uncle Harold walked across the store and locked the front door, then he turned the open sigh around to say closed.

Nico raised his eyebrows in shock, he had never seen his aunt or uncle close the shop early.

The three of them, Nico, his Aunt Eden, and Uncle Harold, sat in almost complete silence, sipping their coffee absently. Occasionally, one or all three would stare at the single cup of coffee still in the holder—the steam no longer snaking up from the open slot.

Nico checked his phone every minute or two, expecting each notification he got to be from Mina. But with each one, he grew more worried when they weren't.

After over an hour passed, and Aunt Eden turned him. "Nico, go out looking for her. Your uncle and I will stay here and let you know if she comes."

"Thank you, Aunt Eden." Nico gave his aunt and uncle hugs before he headed out.

He decided the next best place to check for her was her dorm. So, he texted Autumn a brief explanation of what was happening.

Autumn replied that Mina wasn't in the room, but he should come over and wait with her until she came back.

When Nico got there, Autumn said, "I'm sure something just came up with one of her classes, or she lost track of time. You know she's not good with time—no spatial awareness with that one."

Nico shrugged, unconvinced. They sat on the floor to wait, both looking at the open door hopefully every time someone walked past.

After an hour, Autumn rose and grabbed her phone off the bed. "We should call the police."

"Don't you have to wait a little longer than a few hours to report a missing person?" Nico wasn't sure what the process was for something like this.

"Yeah, I think so." Autumn typed 911 into her phone and hit send. "But I think with the circumstances—the stalking and mugging—they'll look into it."

Not knowing what else to do, he waited for the police to answer, then explained the situation.

"A car has been dispatched to drive the area where she was last seen, and another will inquire at the coffee shop," said the woman on the phone. "Stay in the dorm in case she returns. One of the officers will speak to you shortly."

"Yes, ma'am." All the hope he felt when the police stated they'd look for her, sent him on an emotional rollercoaster. *What if she's just out and lost track of time?*

Deep down, though, he had a sinking feeling, one he couldn't shake.

"What if something's happened to her?" His head hung low.

"We'll find her." Autumn gave him a reassuring hug. "You'll see."

He nodded, then sighed. "I just hope they find her before it gets dark." The thought of her alone and scared weighed heavy on him.

21

Mina Beth Lu

Someone slipped the blindfold off her head, and Mina blinked, trying to get her eyes to adjust to the low light of the room.

She wiggled her fingers but couldn't move her wrists because the duct-tape kept them restrained and tied to a chair. Behind her head was a stone wall. The room looked like a regular basement.

Am I in someone's house? She chewed on the thought.

"So," said a low voice. "What is so special about you?"

Mina turned her head and saw a small but stocky man sitting on a plastic chair by the door.

"You're pretty." He looked Mina up and down. "I can see why you're so important."

"Where am I?" Mina's voice shook.

The man laughed. "Somewhere safe and isolated."

Mina knew he didn't mean safe for her, but *safe* from being disturbed. She looked around but didn't see anyone else in the basement. There were only a few other chairs, and a small table with nothing on it. She couldn't see anything that would help her escape, or any exit other than the one door the man was sitting by.

"Who are you? What do you want?" She'd heard about things like this, and how important it was to establish a line of communication with a kidnapper.

"Don't worry," the man laughed. "I'm not gonna hurt ya."

Despite his words, Mina still felt a chill run down her back.

"Once I get paid, and turn you over, you'll be someone else's problem."

"Paid? By whom?" She paused a moment. "My name's Mina Beth Lu. What's your name?"

The guy just shrugged and stayed silent. The door opened, and another man walked in. He whispered something to her captor sitting in the chair and then left again.

"Seems like there's been a bit of a delay." Her captor leaned back in his chair, making a show of causally settling in. "The boss decided you're worth more than the original deal."

She tried to remain calm but couldn't control her shaking. *Keep him talking.*

"More than the original deal? That's what your boss said, uhm, what did you say his name was?"

"I didn't say." The stocky man seemed to find the conversation funny, and he smiled at her.

Mina wanted to scream but realized it probably wouldn't do her any good. Plus, she didn't want to make the men angry. They were so much bigger than she was and had got her into the basement despite her struggling and trying to fight back.

All she could do was hope someone was looking for her.

She knew Nico expected her at the coffee shop, and his

aunt and uncle would notice when she didn't show up for her shift.

How much time has passed, she wondered? *Is anyone looking for me yet.*

22

Nico Fratelli

"My butt hurts." Autumn straightened her back and rubbed her neck.

They had been sitting for hours on the floor of the dorm. When she called the police again, for an update, Nico had shut the door, not wanting to draw extra attention to what was happening. He still had some hope left that Mina was just on a long walk or had lost track of time in the practice rooms.

Nico checked his watch, then looked out the window. He knew that it had been way too long for Mina to have just gotten caught up in something minor. An overwhelming sensation of fear gripped him.

She's in trouble, I just know it. Nico stood up and started pacing around the room.

"I just need to do something, you know?" Nico said to Autumn.

Autumn nodded, poking at the carpet. "I feel the same way."

"Should we go out looking for her?" Nico wasn't sure how much longer he could stare at the walls of the dorm room.

"I don't know." Autumn stood, then stretched. "What if she comes back here looking for us? She didn't have her keys that last time she was mugged. What if she can't get in? What if she lost her phone?" Autumn twisted the ends of her hair anxiously.

"One of us should stay here." Nico continued to pace.

"I'll stay."

"Are you sure?"

"Yeah, it should be me." Autumn shrugged. "It's my room, after all."

"Okay." Nico was nervous, unsure of how to even formulate a plan for finding Mina.

Where do I look first? He wasn't sure what he would do if she was okay, and just hadn't wanted to see him.

"Call me every thirty minutes, or else I'm gonna send out a search party to look for you. And I don't need to rescue two people." Autumn laughed nervously.

Nico smiled. "Don't worry, I'll be okay."

Autumn nodded, but still looked anxious. "Swear it?" She held up her little pinky.

Nico pulled her into a hug, then looped his pinky with hers. "I swear."

Walking out of the dorm room, Nico felt some guilt. He knew sitting around was the wrong thing to do, but he couldn't help feeling bad about leaving Autumn. She was just as worried about Mina missing as he was, and now she had to sit there alone, not knowing what was happening outside.

For most of their lives, Nico and Autumn had been together through everything bad or stressful. They were used to handling things together. It was Autumn who had comforted Nico on all those birthdays that he didn't hear anything from his mom, and it was Nico who made Autumn feel at home as a freshman when she followed him to college.

When he stepped outside the building, Nico felt how alone he was. He had no idea where to even start looking for Mina. When he had been sitting at the coffee shop, he hadn't seen any sign of her. And if she had been close, he would have seen her on the walk to the music shop.

Nico thought about what Aunt Eden always said when he had lost something.

Retrace your steps. Where did you last see it? Or in this case, her.

He knew that this wasn't exactly the best way to try to find a person, though. The last time he had seen Mina was the day before, and the last place both Nico and Autumn had seen her was her dorm room.

Nico thought about retracing her steps. Autumn said that Mina was still asleep when she left for class in the morning but was gone when Autumn got back from her morning shift at the store. There was a wide gap of time in between when Autumn left for class and when she came home, but somewhere in there was the time that Mina was supposed to meet Nico for coffee.

He made his way back to the coffee shop, hoping that's where Mina had gone.

The sky was slowly starting to darken, so he walked as quickly as he could. If he didn't find Mina before the sun went down, it would get even harder.

With every step, Nico looked around. He didn't even know what he would find but knew that it was better than doing nothing. Every single movement sent his heart racing, hoping that he would find Mina, that she had just gotten the time for their coffee date wrong, or she had gotten stuck talking to Harris or Dustin but was ultimately unharmed.

He was even hoping he would find her out on a walk, avoiding him, because she didn't want to grab a coffee and had been avoiding places, she thought he might be, like the music shop and her dorm room. Even her never wanting to see him again would be a relief compared to the panic he was feeling at the thought of her missing.

Nico turned his head at every beetle that crawled across the sidewalk, every reflection of a flying bird in a shop window, every small echo made by his own footsteps.

Street lamps started to flick on, and Nico was starting to think he should give up. He hadn't received any texts from Autumn, so he figured she was having the same experience he was.

Just as Nico had decided to start making his way back to the dorm, he saw a figure walk into an alleyway across the street. Nico paused, wondering why this person had drawn his attention. As he had been searching, he passed a few people on the sidewalk, but after a quick glance to make sure it wasn't Mina, he kept moving.

Something about this one person in particular was familiar, though. Nico pretended he was looking down at his phone and turned his body, so it would be hard for the person to see his face, if he happened to look around.

The figure started to fade into the darkness of the alley, and Nico was debating anxiously if he should follow.

Would that be insane? Am I overreacting?

He didn't even know who this person was, and it was unlikely he would lead him to Mina.

Nico shook his head. *I'm really losing it.*

As he took his first step back toward the dorms, Nico heard a familiar ringtone. He jumped and pulled his phone back of his pocket, hoping it was his aunt or Autumn with some news, but his screen was blank.

"Yeah?" Nico heard the man down the alley answer the phone. "I'm on my way."

After that, the man hung up the phone and put it back

into his pocket. Something about the way that he spoke had made Nico even more suspicious.

He tipped his head back, thinking about what Autumn would say if she knew what he was thinking. After a few moments, Nico headed off down the alley, following the man.

After Nico had gotten a few feet into the alley, the man stopped walking and turned to face a large metal door. Nico ducked behind a dumpster and held his breath, worried that he had been spotted. For a few moments, all Nico could hear was the sound of a few passing cars in the distance. The only light shining into the alley came from the shop windows across the street.

The man's phone rang again, and he picked it up. Now that Nico was closer, he could hear the man's voice more clearly.

"I'm outside," the man said into his phone.

Nico paused, suddenly, recognizing where he had heard the voice before. Poking his head out from behind the dumpster, he studied the man's profile.

It can't be, can it? He couldn't see much, but between the sound of the guy's voice and the few features clearly visible under the low light, he knew it was Dustin.

Nico let out a sharp gasp.

Dustin turned slightly, looking down the alley in the direction of the dumpster Nico was hiding behind. So, Nico pressed his hand against his mouth and quickly moved back toward the wall, hoping he hadn't been spotted. Just as Nico started to wonder if he should run, he heard the sound of the metal door creaking open.

Too afraid to risk getting caught, Nico kept hiding against the wall. He heard the metal door shut again, and then the voice of a new man.

"You're not the person we met with," said the new voice.

His tone was both casual and hesitant, as if pretending to be more confident than he was.

"You must mean my father," said Dustin. "I'm the one that's going to be doing the saving."

The saving? For a moment, he wondered if Dustin was actually trying to help Mina, but the tone of his voice sounded more menacing than hopeful.

There was a slight pause before the other man asked, "Do you have the money?"

Nico heard a shuffling sound, and then the man muttering under his breath, counting what Nico assumed was a stack of cash.

"We're gonna need more than this," the man said menacingly.

"What do you mean, more?" Dustin asked. "This is what we agreed on."

Nico heard the panic in Dustin's voice that he was desperately trying to hide.

"Come back when you have twice this." The man slammed the large metal door in Dustin's face.

For a while, Nico couldn't hear anything. Dustin didn't move, didn't call anyone. Just stood there, by the doors. Nico poked his head out, to check if Dustin was still there. He saw Dustin on his phone, where he must have been texting with Harris about the change in terms.

Nico almost didn't believe what he had witnessed. It seemed to come out of one of those crime shows that Autumn always made him watch. He never once imagined this was how actual ransoms played out and had never really believed that Dustin and Harris would be capable of something like this.

Nico knew he had to act quickly to rescue Mina, and to catch Dustin. He pulled out his phone, making sure to angle the screen, so the light wouldn't leak into the dark alley, alerting Dustin to Nico's position.

He texted Autumn everything he had heard but was afraid to leave in case they moved her. And he knew he couldn't call the police himself, so he waited for response.

Autumn immediately replied, "Got it. Calling now."

It only took a few minutes before Nico heard police sirens.

Dustin heard them too, and looked around anxiously, trying to figure out if they were coming for him, or if they were just passing by. As the sirens got closer, Dustin started backing up slowly down the alley. When the lights of the police cars started appearing, Dustin took off running.

The police came entered the alley, and Nico slowly came out of his hiding place.

"He's over there." Nico pointed in the direction Dustin had run.

Dustin had gotten out of the alley and had turned somewhere, so he was no longer visible. Some of the officers ran in that direction after him, and one of the police cars left the alley to patrol the street, hoping to catch him.

Nico walked over to the other police cars and started to give them more information about what had happened.

Officers broke through the lock on the metal door and began to file in. Several minutes later, they walked out of the door, holding men in handcuffs. In total, the police brought out three guys from the building, but none of the men they took into custody were Dustin or Harris.

Nico swore at himself, thinking about how he should have known earlier that Dustin would be dangerous. He felt like he should have been able to catch this earlier and regretted not thinking that Dustin or Harris would be capable of something like this.

The officers were talking to Nico, telling him about how he would likely have to testify in court and needed to come back to the police office for more questions about what he knew.

He was so caught up in the procedural aspects, he almost didn't notice the police officers escorting Mina out of the building.

When Mina saw Nico, she ran past the officers to get to him.

"Nico," her voice cracked.

"I was so worried about you." Nico pulled her into a hug, and she wrapped her arms around his neck.

23

Mina Beth Lu

Despite the urgent begging of Nico, Autumn, and her mother, Mina wanted to just return to her life as normal.

The reason she had gotten into all of this mess was because she didn't want to give up her chances of success in college. She knew that happened didn't really change any of that and didn't want to give up on her dreams and ambitions because some men she came into contact with turned out to be monsters.

Sure, she was still a bit uneasy when a stranger's gaze lingered longer than was comfortable, but she had to move on. *I can't let them win.*

Mina knew the advantages Harris had given her were things she could earn back in time with hard work and dedication. Despite the fact Harris mostly just wanted to use her, she was confident in her talent as a musician.

Music's the thing in life she understands best. Without her studies, she would be feeling even more lost.

Her friends and family didn't fully understand why Mina wanted to go back to school after taking just a week off, but they told her they'd support her. She could continue to go to classes and would be able to keep her job at the music shop.

After everything that had happened with Harris, the school offered her free tuition for the rest of her senior year. She knew this was too good of an opportunity to refuse and was worried they might not offer it again if she delayed her graduation.

Even though Mina projected confidence to her friends and family, she was still incredibly nervous about going back to class. The school had been able to replace Harris with another music professor on short notice, so she didn't even have to change her schedule. But that did almost nothing to help her stop shaking at the thought of stepping outside of the safety of her dorm room.

The brush in her hand shook, making it hard to brush out her hair. She knew she would have to leave for class in just a few minutes. A quick walk to the shuttle, and a ride over would keep her around people and in plain view.

Wham. The door to her room hit the wall and made Mina jump.

"Oh, sorry," said Autumn. "Didn't mean to startle you."

Mina laughed nervously. "It's okay, you didn't startle me."

Autumn gave Mina an unconvinced look. "You don't have to pretend like that, you know. It's fine to be a bit jumpy, especially after all that's happened."

Mina shrugged. "I guess I'm kind of nervous." She didn't want to say anything that would make Autumn worry any more than she already was.

What had happened with Dustin had been hard on other people, too, and her choice to come back to school was putting some stress on all of the people who cared about her.

Autumn had told her a million times, all that mattered was what she wanted for herself, and what other people felt about it shouldn't factor into Mina's choices. But Mina had spent the last week with her mom, who had then cried when Mina hugged her goodbye just the night before.

"Do you need anything?" Autumn rested her hip against Mina's desk.

"No, I'm okay," replied Mina.

"You sure?" Autumn shot her a sisterly look. "Want me to walk with you to the shuttle?"

"No. I'm good." Mina tried her best to put on a reassuring smile for Autumn but wasn't sure how convincing she had managed to be. "I gotta jump back into the swing of things."

If she was being completely honest, Mina was afraid. There wasn't a good way anyone could keep her safe, especially since Dustin and Harris hadn't been found yet. As far as Mina knew, the police had some leads and were looking into them. There were rumors that Dustin and Harris had run to a different country or had changed their identities. But nothing was confirmed, and all the possible scenarios were only that, scenarios.

I don't really have anything to worry about. They're gonna catch them, and pretty soon. And when the police apprehended them, she would testify against them in court.

All Mina wanted was to never have to think about them again. But there were some other, more worrisome rumors Mina was thinking about. A few people reported seeing either Harris or Dustin around the town. There were conflicting stories about it, with some people saying they had dyed their hair, or had grown beards, and others who said that none of their looks had changed. People saw Harris and Dustin in the grocery store, in the car passing them in the other lane, walking past their house at night—the sightings were relentless.

"Well, I'm here if you need me." Autumn sat on the floor and rested her head against Mina's leg.

Mina couldn't help but smile, thinking about how lucky

she had gotten to have Autumn as a roommate. Even though things had been chaotic since the day that they had first met, Autumn never questioned helping Mina.

"Thank you." Mina ran some gloss over her lips.

"For what?" Autumn tilted her head.

"I don't know." Mina shrugged. "Just because."

Autumn checked her phone. "Are you heading out soon?"

"Yeah." Mina put up her makeup and hairbrush back into a drawer. "I'm going to be late, at this point."

"Hey." Autumn put a hand on her shoulder. "Let me know when you get there, okay?"

"Sure." Mina smiled at Autumn over her shoulder, then she walked out of the room.

She knew Autumn was just worried, and this was a good way to make Autumn feel better about Mina being outside. But Mina didn't like anything that reminded her of what had happened. And when people asked for her to let them know she was safe, it only made her more nervous to be walking around alone.

Dustin and Harris had become a sort of local legend in the town. So, as Mina walked to class, she felt the eyes of passing students watching her. On the bus, someone stood up, so that she could have a seat.

Why can't my life go back to normal? She had enough to deal with after the abduction, but now, she also had to hear about it everywhere she went.

She couldn't be Mina the music major, the violinist. She was "that girl." It seemed like just as things were starting to look up for her, she had suddenly gained some sort of celebrity out of being a victim.

Walking back up the stairs of Lewis Hall for the first time since Harris had been gone, Mina felt another wave of anxiety. She considered, for a moment, just turning around and walking to her dorm. But she knew she'd have to go eventually and didn't want to put it off any further.

The front door seemed heavier, harder for Mina to open.

Is it new, or has it always been this way? She hadn't noticed before.

The hallways echoed with life like she'd remembered, and the building seemed vacant this close to class time.

At least the inside of the building hasn't changed.

When Mina walked in through the doors to the classroom, she was reminded of the first time that semester, she had walked in. Taking a deep breath, she hoped the professor wouldn't make a scene like Harris had when she walked in late.

As she opened the door, Mina hoped it would be an entirely different experience.

Instead of already playing, the professor was sitting with the other musicians, just talking.

Mina couldn't hear what they were saying, but she could feel how relaxed the energy of the room was. It was completely opposite to how she had felt walking in late to the first day of Harris' class, when everyone had already been playing.

The professor sat in a regular chair with the students. When Mina walked in, the professor turned around to look at her. She had a calming look, with long grey hair and glasses on a pearl string around her neck. Mina smiled at her and introduced herself.

"Sorry I'm late, I'm Mina Beth Lu." She kept walking toward the chairs, having seen an empty one just a few feet away from where the professor was sitting.

"Oh, Mina. Welcome. I'm Professor Sylvia Rosa." The professor stood to greet her.

"Nice to meet you too." She kept her head bowed, unable to make eye contact.

When Mina was close enough, Professor Rosa reached out a hand to shake Mina's. "Take a seat," she said warmly.

"We're just talking about what we all might be interested in playing for the rest of the semester."

"Great," said Mina quietly, still a little shy about being late.

"Why don't you stay behind for a few moments when class is over, so I can catch you up on what you've missed."

At the sound of her words to remain after class, fear made every muscle in her body tense, and she blinked back the urge to cry. It was the same thing Harris had said to her on that first day.

For the rest of the period, the students sat in a circle and talked. Mina had never seen this happen in a music class before, and she could tell her other classmates were surprised as well. By the end of it, they had picked out a few pieces to try during the following class.

"I'll email everyone copies of the selected music," said Professor Rosa. "So, each of you can practice a bit before playing together."

Mina stayed in her seat as everyone else filed out. When the last person had left the room and closed the door, Professor Rosa turned to talk to Mina.

"Mina, I don't want to make you uncomfortable, but I was told about what had happened to you with the previous director of this class." Professor Rosa paused.

Mina pulled on the ends of her hair nervously.

Professor Rosa continued, "I just think what he did was awful, and I want to try to make it up to you." She smiled at Mina. "I know that I didn't have anything to do with it, but I want to make sure that someone with as much talent as you, doesn't fall out of love with music because of people like him."

Mina nodded, unsure of what to say.

Professor Rosa stood and walked across the room to a cabinet that was tucked against the far wall. She pulled out a folder and walked back over to the chairs.

"Now, I know that there might be some safety concerns with you performing in the concert at the end of the semester, with the rest of the class."

"Yes." Mina nodded. "The police don't have Harris' location. They said that he might try to contact me again."

"I don't want you to feel pressured to do this if you don't want to. But I think we can turn this problem into a new opportunity for you." Professor Rosa opened the folder and handed Mina a few papers.

She looked at the papers, surprised to find they were blank music scores.

"What do you mean?" Confusion etched her mind.

"What about, instead of playing with your class, you compose their music? I've been looking for an assistant to help me with a project, but I haven't found the right person until I heard about you."

Mina was shocked. This had been the last thing she had expected when Professor Rosa asked her to stay after class.

"Wow," said Mina. "Are you sure?"

"I'm absolutely certain." Professor Rosa laughed and nodded.

"Thank you." She had a hard containing her excitement.

"So, that's a yes?"

"Most definitely." Mina stood up and shook Professor Rosa's hand.

"I'm so glad. Oh, I have a music studio in my home, it's where I conduct private music lessons—have for years." A warm smile stretched across her lips. "On the back of the first page, you'll find my address. Why don't you stop by tomorrow, say around five or six, and we'll talk about the specifics?"

"That sounds great." Mina grabbed her violin case and slung her bag over her shoulder.

"Okay, well, I'll see you then." Professor Rosa nodded, which Mina took as her que to leave.

As Mina walked out the door, she turned to tell Professor Rosa one last, "Thank you."

24

Nico Fratelli

The bell on the shop door rang.

Nico looked up and smiled, watching Mina walked in. He tried to downplay his smile when her eyes met his, but he couldn't help it. Every time he saw her, he felt a weight lift off his shoulders. Nico knew she was safe now, but it would take a lot longer than a week for him to forget about what had happened.

Mina walked over to Nico at the register.

"I didn't know you were gonna be here today." She leaned her elbows on the counter and smiled up at him.

"Oh, I just had some free time." Nico laughed, trying to act casual even though his heart was beating so fast, he could hear it.

The truth was that when Nico had some free time, he tended to stay as far away from the shop as he could. He already worked most nights, so he spent his few days off hanging out with Autumn until the shop closed. But he knew

Mina would be working during the last few hours of the day, and he figured it wouldn't hurt to be there and see her.

Plus, it was Monday, which is when his band practiced. They always met in the back room of the music shop. It was usually deserted, so that they could have some privacy while they worked on new songs.

Nico figured it wouldn't do him any harm to get there a few hours earlier than he usually would have, if it meant he could spend some time with Mina.

"How long are you gonna be here?" Mina organized the student music books in the woodwind section. "Maybe we could walk back to campus together?"

"I'll be here until closing. My band practices in the back room on Thursdays, so I just help out around the shop until then." Nico's heart raced. "If you want to stay and hang out while we practice, we can walk back together."

Nico busied himself by organizing the pens on the counter, so that they were all facing the same way, and the ends lined up.

"You have a band? What's it called?"

Nico laughed. "We're not that serious. It's just for fun."

"Oh, good." Mina moved to the brass book section.

"Good?" Nico froze, worried about what Mina was thinking.

Mina covered her face with her hands. "Ah, I didn't mean it like that." She nervously fiddled with the boxed strings for the violins. "It's just that it can be hard to do things only for fun. And it's nice you have that."

"Don't you do anything just for fun?" Nico moved closer and fixed the saxophone reeds on a spinning tower.

Mina shrugged. "I guess. Sometimes I watch movies and stuff."

"Watching things doesn't count as a hobby."

"Well, that's not fair." Mina pouted. "All you asked about was doing things for fun."

Nico smiled and leaned his elbow on the counter. "Okay then, so what about your hobbies?"

Mina tilted her head. "Violin?"

"Nope." Nico laughed. "It doesn't count if it's what you study."

Confusion washed across the delicate lines of her face.

"What is it?"

"I've seen you in the orchestra room, but I've never seen you play. What instrument do you, uhm, do you . . ."

"Cello is my primary instrument. But I'm in for a music teaching degree. It's something my aunt says I can fall back on in life. Plus, I could teach lessons here too, like she does if I wanted, so could you now that I think about it."

"Maybe when I have more time, or even during winter or summer break some time."

An awkward silence fell between them. And it was then he realized she had changed the subject.

"So, back to hobbies . . ."

"I don't know." She chewed on her lower lip and looked as if deep in thought. "I guess. I put most of my time into making sure I do everything I have to do."

Nico leaned against the counter, hoping he looked cool. "Okay, I'm gonna give you an assignment."

Mina laughed. "Yeah? What's that?"

"This weekend, you have to do something for fun."

Mina rolled her eyes.

"No, I'm serious. Look, Autumn and I are going to a party on Saturday. You should come."

"I've been to parties. They're not really my thing."

"Yeah, but you haven't been to parties with me and Autumn. Trust me, it'll be fun."

"Fine. But for the record, my agreement is reluctant. And I want to be back home and in fuzzy socks by midnight."

"Got it," Nico smiled, already thinking about what he was going to wear.

A woman and her son, middle grade age, entered the shop.

Mina walked around the counter. "Now, I have some work to do."

On her way over to the storefront where the customers were, Mina pushed one of the pens Nico had been fidgeting with out of line.

The rest of the workday went by as normal. Nico had called his aunt and uncle to let them know he would be coming in, so they took the afternoon off. It was just Nico and Mina in the shop once the woman and her son left.

Nico kept checking the clock, and for once, it wasn't because he was counting down the time until the shop closed. He was nervous about Mina staying for his band's practice. They usually didn't have people who came and watched, and only had a few real gigs outside of just playing in the back of the shop. It seemed like time was going too quickly, and as the minutes ticked by Nico became increasingly anxious.

It seemed like only minutes had passed between when Mina first came in and when Nico's bandmates, Robin, and Luca, showed up for practice. As they set up, Nico watched Mina take a seat against the wall. He could tell she felt a little out of place, and she was nervously tapping her fingers against her knee.

As Luca unpacked his guitar, he looked at Mina. "So, how do you know Nico?"

"I'm Autumn's roommate," Mina said nervously.

Robin started to tune his bass. "So, how'd you end up here?"

"Sorry?" Mina's eyes widened.

Robin glanced at Nico and smirked. "If you're just Autumn's roommate, how'd you end up here?"

"Oh, well . . ." Mina started to answer, but didn't know how to respond.

"Hey," said Nico. "Take it easy with all the questions, guys. I'll be right back."

Nico went into the bathroom to splash some water onto his face. He looked into the mirror and tried to imagine himself confident, but he was still uneasy as he walked back into the room.

By the time Nico had returned, Robin, Luca, and Mina were laughing at something together.

"What'd I miss?" Nico checked the door, making sure it was locked.

The three of them looked at Nico and paused for a moment.

"Nothing," said Luca, in a way that made Nico think they had been talking about him.

Nico cleared his throat. "Should we get started then?"

"Waiting on you." Robin tested the sound and recording systems.

Nico slid a chair over to make a half-circle with Robin and Luca, facing Mina. Cello in hand, he matched the modern-day sound of his bandmates. He felt a little awkward when the band first started playing, and especially when his singing parts came in. He had sung in front of plenty of people before, and Autumn sat in on their practices a lot, so it wasn't like he had stage fright. It was just Mina was there, and it felt different.

It seemed like the more he tried to forget the room and focus on the song, the worse he did. After only thirty minutes of practice, Nico decided to call it.

"Hey, I'm feeling a little tired, are you guys okay if we end early?" He wiped down his cello.

Robin and Luca agreed and started to pack up their stuff. Nico figured they could probably tell he had been feeling a little off during practicing and felt embarrassed. Once they were ready to leave, Nico walked them out the front door of the shop, so he could lock it after they left.

"Get some rest," called Luca over his shoulder, then he and Robin walked away.

Nico locked the door and turned around to find Mina standing behind the counter, grabbing her bag and her jacket.

"Want me to walk you home?" A jittery, nervous energy make him feel jumpy.

"Sure." Mina smiled.

The sun had set about an hour earlier, and Nico could tell Mina was a little bit on edge. He fought the urge to reach out and hold her hand or link her arm through his, worried that it would make her feel more uncomfortable rather than protected.

"Sorry the practice was a little lackluster there." He tried to hide his embarrassment.

"No, it was great. Thanks for letting me sit in." Mina smiled, but Nico knew she was a talented musician, and as such, would have known he had been off during practice—singing off-key.

"I was just a little nervous tonight. I promise the next time you hear us, it'll go better." Nico laughed.

"Nervous? About what?"

Nico paused, unsure of how to answer the question. If he was honest and told Mina, he was nervous because he had wanted to impress her, he was risking a lot. Especially after what happened to her. He didn't want her to feel uncomfortable. And he worried she would feel as if she had to go along with whatever he said because she felt indebted to him, just like she had felt indebted to Harris.

But if he never said anything, then he wouldn't have a chance with her at all.

Before Nico could decide whether or not he should tell Mina about how he felt, Mina spoke.

"Was it me?" she asked softly.

Nico felt his entire face turn white. Never in his life had

he felt this much panic before. He couldn't tell if her tone was hopeful or hesitant and was quickly running out of time to deliver a smooth reply.

"Yes," said Nico. Hearing it out loud only made him panic more. In the few seconds that followed, he replayed that one word in his head a hundred times, wishing he had just brushed it off.

Instead of waiting another agonizing second for Mina to reply, Nico awkwardly changed the subject.

"You're still up for that party with Autumn and I on Saturday?"

"Y-yeah," stuttered Mina. "Sounds like fun."

Nico knew she was lying when she said that she thought it would be fun. He worried this was her way of trying to move past what he had said. They continued the rest of the walk making small talk. But Nico couldn't stop thinking about tonight, and if Mina had rejected him or if it was just a misunderstanding.

When they got to Mina's dorm, Nico stopped by the stairs. Every other time Nico had walked Mina home, she had stayed back to talk to him for a minute before heading inside. This time, Mina just continued up the stairs and opened the door.

"Goodnight," Mina called over her shoulder.

"Goodnight." Nico watched her until she disappeared from view.

Mina Beth Lu

Mina hadn't seen or talked to Nico since the night he had walked her home after his band's practice. It had only been two days, but that was plenty of time for Mina to replay the few hours over and over in her head. She wondered if she had offended him in some way, and worried about how he had suddenly switched his tone when they were walking back to her dorm.

Mina was afraid to ask Autumn about it but had confirmed with her earlier in the morning that the three of them were still going out to the party later. Autumn hadn't been acting weirdly around Mina since Thursday, so Mina tried to tell herself that everything was okay, and Nico wasn't upset with her.

Her roommate was always blunt and honest. Mina knew if she asked her for advice, Autumn would probably be able to help.

It was getting closer and closer to the time they were supposed to meet up with Nico and head over to the party.

Mina looked over at Autumn, who was sitting on her bed, playing a game on her phone.

"Hey, Autumn?"

"Yeah?" She looked up from her phone.

"Ah, it's nothing, never mind." Mina busied herself with fixing her makeup, even though she had already finished applying everything.

Just blurt it out already, she scolded herself in silence.

Even though Autumn was likely more loyal to Nico, Mina was sure she would, at least, try to help Mina understand what was going on.

"Ah, he's here." Autumn jumped off her bed and pulled on a light jacket. "Ready?"

Mina nodded but felt more nauseated than ready.

When they got outside, Nico met her and Autumn with a smile. "Hi, Mina."

"Hey." She tried to sound casual but worried her tone had come off as panicked.

"How are you?" Nico pulled the zipper of his jacket up and down.

"Oh, I'm fine." Mina smiled. "How're you? It's been a few days."

"Yeah, I've just been a little busy with class work." Nico rubbed the back of his head nervously. "And some score work with my band—a solo."

"Wait, for a cello?"

"No. For base. I play all stringed instruments, but base is my favorite."

Hmm. How did I not know this?

"Hey," Autumn cut in. "Do either of you two lovebirds know where we're supposed to be headed?"

Mina felt her face flush with warmth, and when she glanced at Nico, he was apple red.

"Y-yeah." Nico cleared this throat. "The apartment's down by the water tower."

Autumn nodded and walked a few steps ahead of them, leading the way.

Silence fell between her and Nico, and they both took turns stealing nervous glances.

Mina's breath coming out in clouds, lingering in front of her. She hadn't anticipated it would be this cold out, surprised to remember it was already fall. It had only been a week or so, but temperature was quickly dropping, and nights were always cooler.

Mina shivered a little and crossed her arms to keep warm.

Nico glances at her, but this time, he didn't look away. She smiled at him, not really knowing what to say.

"Are you cold?" Nico unzipped his garment. "Do you, uhm . . . want to borrow my jacket?"

Mina hesitated, unsure whether or not he actually meant it.

Goosebumps started to form under her sleeves, and she thought longingly about how warm his jacket looked. She thought about what it would be like to wear it, wanting its warmth but also wanting to know what it would feel like to wear his clothes, to smell his scent so close.

Mina was growing sick of having to overthink everything, especially when it came to Nico. She wondered if the two of them would be somewhere else if she hadn't always been so hesitant around him.

"Yeah." Mina found her voice and held his gaze. "If you don't mind."

Mina was surprised when Nico looked really happy. He even seemed to try to suppress his smile, like he was trying to downplay how glad he was to let her borrow his jacket.

As Nico took his jacket off, a shadow pass across the glow of a porch light.

Mina stopped and glanced around, but she couldn't see anyone.

"What is it?" Nico handed Mina his jacket.

She took the jacket and slipped it on. "Nothing, just got spooked by a shadow."

Once Mina was warm, the walk felt a lot shorter. Wearing Nico's jacket made her feel safer, somehow, like it was a shield instead of just worn-out flannel.

"This it?" Autumn called suddenly.

Startled, Mina yelped followed by a noticeable jump.

"You okay?" Autumn's brows knit together in concern.

Mina laughed it off. "Yeah, just nerves."

"I didn't realize we were here." Nico looked up at her.

There was no question they were in the right place. Dim lights flashed through the windows of an apartment on the second floor and music drifted out of the same open windows.

Walking up the steps to the party, Mina felt nervous. Parties didn't usually make her feel that way, she just didn't usually have fun at them. This time, Mina felt like there was something looming over her head. She knew she hadn't been able to adjust to being outside of familiar spaces yet, but she was with Nico and Autumn, who she trusted to keep her safe.

Mina did her best to shrug off the feeling.

"I'm thirsty." Autumn grabbed her hand and pulled her over to a table full of drinks.

Nico was swept away by a few of his band members.

Mina recognized Robin and Luca from the band, as well as a few other people she had seen around the music department before.

Autumn noticed Mina looking over at Nico. "He'll be back, don't worry."

Mina nodded and smiled, trying to at least seem like she was enjoying the party for Autumn's sake.

"Do you want to dance?" Autumn swayed to the music.

Mina shook her head, thinking about how ridiculous she

would feel dancing in that crowd of mostly unfamiliar faces. She hadn't even finished her first drink yet.

"Maybe later." Mina took another sip.

Autumn shrugged. "It means a lot to him you came out tonight."

"What?"

"To Nico," Autumn shouted over the music. "He's been really worried about you. We all have."

"I know, I'm sorry." Mina clutched her drink in both hands.

"No. No." Autumn shook her head. "Don't be sorry. It's not your fault. None of it. You hear me?"

"Yeah," Mina said, unconvinced.

"Stop blaming yourself for what they did. Okay?"

Mina shrugged. She knew that it wasn't logical, but all she could think about was how she should have acted differently, and how she could have probably put a stop to everything that happened if she had tried harder. Tears pooled in the corners of her eyes.

"Oh, Mina." Autumn pulled her into a hug. "It's not your fault."

Mina bit her lip, holding back the flood of emotions.

Autumn gave her a reassuring smile. "Let's just have fun, all right?"

Mina laughed, breaking the heaviness of the conversation. "Yeah, I'd like that."

She and Autumn stood off to the side of the party together.

Mina finished her first drink, then her second and third. Autumn was pointing out all the people who she didn't like, telling Mina the gossip and rumors behind almost everyone at the party. Her laughter was lost in noise, no one could hear her over the music. Mina felt like she was wrapped in a blanket, and for the first time since the abduction, she was able to let go of her fears.

While talking to Autumn, she kept an eye on Nico. He was still across the room, talking to some of his friends. Every once in a while, he would glance over at her, and she would quickly look away, so he wouldn't know that she had been staring at him. It looked like every time he tried to break away from his conversation to rejoin her and Autumn, his friends pulled him back in.

Mina was so engrossed in her conversation with Autumn, and with watching Nico, the sounds around her faded into the background.

"Fire." A shout came from somewhere at the back of the room. "Fire. The house is on fire."

She'd been so focused on Autumn and Nico that did pickup on the burning smell. Her stung, and she blinked several times. When she refocused, everyone was running.

"Come on," Autumn shouted by her ear.

Smoke billowed into the room, making it hard to breathe. She took two steps, following Autumn, then slammed into someone.

The crowd stampeded past, shoving her against the wall.

Mina lost track of Autumn and Nico in the confusion, and desperately looked around the room for them.

Someone grabbed her arm and tugged.

"Nico, the doors that way," she shouted, then pointed.

When she looked up, it was Dustin she locked eyes with.

"No." Fear made her chest constrict. "No. No. No."

He dragged her in the direction of the smoke.

Mina screamed for help, but it got lost in the chaos of the room.

Nico Fratelli

The second Nico realized there was a fire in the apartment, he rushed toward where he had last seen Mina and Autumn. He had to fight against the flow of people trying to leave the building, and by the time he got there, they were both gone. Panicked, he looked around, hoping to catch sight of them.

"Nico!" He turned around to see Autumn. She held his arm and said, "I lost Mina."

"Get outside," said Nico. "I'll find her."

Autumn nodded and ran. He knew there was no time for hesitation. The fire was getting closer, and the apartment was filling up with smoke. It had only been a few minutes since the fire started, but it was already hard to breathe.

Nico pulled his shirt over his face to create a filter, hoping it would help him last longer in the smoke. As the room started to clear out, Nico knew Mina wasn't there. She wasn't in the crowd of people bottlenecking at the door, either. So, where was she?

The smoke was most dense around the entrance to the

kitchen. Nico started to walk slowly in that direction, hoping he had been wrong and that Mina had somehow made it out of the apartment.

As he entered the kitchen, Nico saw a shadow move against the far corner, where the smoke was the thickest.

"Mina?" Without hesitating, Nico ran forward.

He thought he heard some sort of muffled reply. The closer he got, the clearer the figure became. Nico squinted his eyes against the smoke and reached out. When he was just two steps away, Nico paused. He realized, it wasn't just one figure in front of him, it was two.

"Nico," shouted Mina, lunging toward him. The other figure held her back by her arm and was dragging her toward the door that led out to the back porch.

Nico reached out for Mina, holding her arm, and prying the other person's hand off her. All three of them were coughing in the smoke.

The moment the other person released Mina's arm, he turned and ran out the back door.

Nico laced his fingers with Mina's, then together, they bolted through the apartment to the front door and down the stairs.

Once they were in the fresh air, Nico leaned over, trying to catch his breath.

Most of the people who were at the party had run off, but a few stayed behind, hovering on the sidewalk, and watching as the flames spread.

The sound of sirens grew, and in a few moments, fire-fighters were pouring into the building.

Mina tugged on Nico's sleeve to get his attention. "It was Dustin," she said softly in his ear.

"What?" Nico liked the way their hands fit together. "Are you okay?"

Mina nodded. "I think he set the fire. He must have followed us."

"Nico? Mina?" Autumn ran up and greeted both of them with a big hug. "You should get checked out by paramedics. You were both in there for a long time."

"I feel fine now." Nico held on to Mina, not wanting to release her hand.

Mina nodded as well.

"Mina, I tried to find you, but you were just gone. I'm so sorry I left you. I didn't mean to—" Autumn's eyes were red and bloodshot from the smoke.

"It's okay," replied Mina. "It's not your fault. It was Dustin's."

Autumn sighed. "Tell me why I'm not surprised. You need to tell the police."

"I will." Mina's voice carried a layer of exhaustion.

"If you want, I can call the detective for you. You'll probably have to call him back tomorrow, but, at least, for now, you can just rest." Autumn looked down at Mina and Nico's hands, then grinned.

"Really? Are you sure?"

Autumn nodded. "It's not a big deal, I've got it." Autumn looked over at Nico. "You'll get her back safe, right?"

Nico nodded. "I will."

Autumn gave them a quick smile before walking off to call the detective.

"Do you want to go back to your dorm?"

"Yeah," Mina said softly.

Nico, still holding her hand, headed back to the dorm.

"Maybe we should call the campus police, too." While he walked, he was on edge, looking around the area.

"But it didn't happen on school grounds." She glanced at him, and her dark lashes fluttered.

"No, but they can maybe keep an eye on your dorm just in case he, uhm . . ."

"Do you think he'll show up there?" A shiver made her

shake, and somehow, he didn't think it was caused by the cool, evening air.

She wasn't the only one feeling stressed by the events of the evening. It was as if Nico expected Dustin to jump out at any moment. At one point, he thought footsteps drummed behind them, but when he turned around, no one was there. Every so often, the sound of crunching leaves, or the wind through the trees, would catch his ear and make his heart race faster than he thought possible.

By the time he and Mina got back to the dorm, Nico was almost certain someone had followed them. He didn't want to scare Mina by mentioning it. But he could tell she had heard the same things as him.

At the stairs to the building, and Mina paused. "Can you come in?"

"Of course." Nico agreed immediately. He wanted to make sure she would be safe.

On the way to Mina's room, Nico's phone buzzed with a text.

"Is it Autumn?"

"Yeah." He nodded. "She's at the police station, telling the detective what happened. She doesn't know when she'll be back. But she said to not worry—she'll take a cab."

"Can you stay with me? At least, until she gets back?"

"Of course." Nico scrolled through his phone contacts and called the campus police.

Once the on-duty officer answered, he explained what had happened, and how Autumn was at the station talking to the detective. Once done, the hung up.

"What'd they say?" She avoided his gaze.

"They're getting in touch with the detective on your case," he said. "And since there was a confirmed sighting of Dustin, and possible arson, extra security detail will keep watch around the dorm."

"That's good, right?"

"Yes. You'll be safe." His words sounded hollow, empty to him, and he felt helpless. He wanted to make her feel safe, protected, comforted, but he wasn't sure what to do.

Once inside Mina's room, he stood awkwardly, not knowing what to do next.

Nico realized he had never been alone with Mina in her room before, and it felt strange that Autumn wasn't there. He looked around, trying to think of something to say, but nothing felt right for the moment.

Mina broke the silence. "Can I ask you something?"

Nico's heart raced, surprised at the question. "What is it?"

"Why did you go looking for me? How did you know where I was?"

"Honestly, I don't know how I found you." Nico shifted his arms, unsure of what to do with them. "I wasn't sure whether you had made it out or not. I couldn't leave without knowing you were safe."

Mina looked at him, and Nico saw tears welling in her eyes. He didn't want her to cry. She had already endured enough sadness in the last week. As Nico looked at her, he realized all he wanted in the world was to be able to make her happy.

"God, Mina, I was so worried." He wrapped one arm around Mina's waist and pulled her closer.

He wiped a stray tear off Mina's cheek with his thumb.

Mina leaned into him, and he cupped her face in his hand.

Don't overthink it, Nico said to himself. He leaned down and kissed her, running his fingers through her silky hair.

Mina stood on her toes, so their heights were more evenly matched.

Embraced in his arms, her body felt right against his. The kiss, slow and tender, made his heart ache.

I could stay like this forever, he thought.

The doorknob rattled, and he jumped back.

"Oh, uh, do you want me to give you a minute?" Autumn's hand hovered on the doorknob.

"No, we're good, sorry." A wave of heat made his face feel flushed.

"Okay then." Autumn walked into the room slowly, as if they would change their mind any second.

"How'd it go?" Mina licked her lips, then took a seat on the edge of her bed.

"Well, nothing really helpful happened tonight. Men went out to search the area, but they came up empty-handed. Detective Fontana wants you to come in tomorrow to tell your side of what you saw." Autumn moved to sit at her desk.

"You look pretty tired, Mina." Nico wasn't sure if he should sit or go. "Do you want me to leave?"

Mina looked hesitant, and she took a moment before speaking. "Yeah, I'm exhausted." She looked over at Autumn, then back at Nico. "But . . . I don't know if it's safe here. I know they have extra security and all, but . . ."

"What do you mean?" Autumn leaned against the back of her chair.

"We might have been followed," said Nico. "But I don't know for sure."

"I never saw anyone. But I heard some footsteps when we were walking back" Mina leaned her back against her bed frame. "I think he followed us to the party, too."

"So, he might know where we live?" Autumn looked out the window nervously.

Nico joined her, but on the third floor, all he could see were tree branches.

"What if he's out there right now?" Autumn whispered, as if Dustin would be able to hear her.

"If you want, I can stay here tonight," said Nico. "I could sleep on the floor. It's a bit late to go somewhere else, and if he's watching us, he would just follow us there."

"Are you sure?" Mina asked.

Nico could hear the relief in her voice, which made him feel even more determined to stay and keep her safe.

"Yeah, it'll be okay just for the night. Tomorrow we can see if there's a better option."

Nico got a pillow from Autumn and a blanket from Mina, laid on the floor, staring at the ceiling. He was exhausted from the night, but once the lights went out, Nico knew that it would be a while before he, or any of them, would be able to fall asleep.

Mina Beth Lu

It was only Mina's second time working with Professor Rosa on composing for her class, and Mina wanted to be able to impress her. She had dressed professionally, and even made it to her office on time. But Mina couldn't stop thinking about when Nico kissed her.

She had seen him a few times after, in the music shop, in her dorm, and for coffee, but they were never alone. Mina kept thinking about how she should go about asking him on a real date, something he had never asked a guy to do before, and there was the added complication of her not being safe outside.

Mina was trying to wait until everything had settled down since Dustin had started the fire. But it didn't seem as if things would end anytime soon. She still didn't have good living arrangements figured out. Moving to a different dorm on campus didn't seem like it would be enough to keep her safe.

Nico had invited her and Autumn to stay with him, so for the past few nights they had slept on the couches in Nico's garage apartment over his aunt's and uncle's place. It was only a temporary solution, but Mina felt stuck. She didn't know anywhere else she would feel protected.

"Mina?" Professor Rosa said, pulling Mina out of her thoughts. "Hello." She waved a hand in front of her face.

"Oh, sorry, Professor." Embarrassment warmed her cheeks.

"You seem like you've been somewhere else all day. Are you feeling all right?"

Mina hesitated, not knowing how much she should share with her professor. She knew she needed to give the woman an explanation as to why she was so distracted, but she didn't want to overshare.

"I'm okay." Mina fixed the papers in her hand. "It's just some things about the investigation."

"What happened? Did they get caught?"

Mina shook her head. "Not yet."

"Then, what is it?" Professor Rosa asked. Noticing Mina's hesitation, Professor Rosa said, "Sorry, you don't have to tell me anything if you're not comfortable. But I would like to know if there's anything I can do to help."

"I don't think there's much anyone can do to help." Mina sighed. "Over the weekend, I think Dustin tried to kill me."

"What?" Professor Rosa sat next to her. "How? When? And why am I just now hearing of this?" Concern etched the woman's eyes.

"I'm fine, don't worry." Mina regretted how she had phrased what had happened. "I'm just looking for a new place to live."

"Why?"

"Because he followed me to my dorm, and I've been living on my friend's couch ever since."

Professor Rosa paused, looking lost in thought.

"I-I'm sorry. I didn't mean to bring it up. I'm fine, really."

Mina wondered if she had said something wrong, and nervously looked back at the few scraps of music that they had managed to put together so far.

"I think I can help you, if you'd like," said Professor Rosa. "I have a spare bedroom in my house that's just collecting dust. You're welcome to stay with me. And the building has security. No gets in or out without the passcode."

"Really? Are you sure?" Mina was shocked. It seemed like the perfect solution to her problems, but she was nervous about imposing on her professor's space.

"I know it's a little unusual to move into your professor's house, but it seems like your situation is difficult right now. You can live there for free for as long as you need to."

"Wow, that sounds incredible," Mina said, relieved.

"It'll be easier for us to work together, too." A warm smile covered her lips. "I have a friend who lives with me, a pianist. He can help us while we work."

"I wouldn't want to put either of you in danger, though." Mina didn't think that Dustin would harm her elderly professor and her professor's friend, but she had learned not to underestimate him.

"I'm sure we'll be okay. Plus, I have a big dog who can act scary when he senses something is wrong," Professor Rosa pulled a notecard out of her desk. "And, you probably won't have to be alone in the house ever. My friend, Vincent, doesn't leave the house much, if at all."

Mina watched Professor Rosa write on a card. When finished, she handed it to her.

"This is my address," said Professor Rosa. "It's only a few blocks from campus. Come by for dinner tonight. You can take a look at the room and meet Vincent and the dog."

"Are you certain this is okay?" Mina was unsure because she really didn't want to impose.

"I'm positive." Professor Rosa smiled warmly.

"I don't know how to thank you for this."

"Well, if you'd like, you can bring a dessert to dinner. Vincent can be a little aloof, but he'll love you instantly if you bring him some sugar cookies."

Mina laughed. "Okay then, sugar cookies it is."

They spent another two hours going over the music. Mina felt comfortable around Professor Rosa, and they worked well together. She knew moving into her home would be weird at first, but she also knew she would eventually get comfortable there. Unlike Harris, it didn't seem like Professor Rosa had any kind of ulterior motive for offering to help Mina above the offering of help.

Later in the afternoon, Mina worked a shift at the music shop. She found herself actually looking forward to the dinner at Professor Rosa's house. When she told Nico about it, he seemed hesitant. Mina knew he just wanted to look out for her, but she was confident she was making the right choice this time.

"I think I've learned enough from what happened with Harris. Professor Rosa isn't like him, though. She's really nice," Mina told Nico. As much as she tried to reassure him, he didn't seem convinced.

"Can you make sure to text me when you get there? And when you leave? And also, maybe at some point in between?" Nico asked, only half joking.

"You don't need to worry about me. It'll be okay, and I promise to text you whenever I have an update of any kind."

"Text me even if the update is just that you didn't like the salad they served." Nico smiled. "Don't worry about bothering me tonight. Message me at any house. I just want to know you're doing okay."

Mina agreed to text him as much as she could during the dinner, feeling safe just knowing he cared.

At the end of her shift, Nico offered to walk her to

Professor Rosa's house. Mina agreed, knowing it would be about a fifteen-minute walk from the music shop. And being alone outside for that long made her nervous.

As they were walking, Nico said, "I know everything's been a bit chaotic recently, but we never did get coffee."

Mina laughed. "No, I guess we didn't."

"If you're free tomorrow, maybe we could do something? Doesn't have to be coffee." He pauses a moment. "I would understand if you didn't want to because of what happened last time."

Mina nodded. She hadn't been able to get over her nerves and going on that walk to the coffee shop again would only remind her of the abducted.

"Let's do something else"

"Great." Nico smiled widely. He looked the other way, as if he didn't want Mina to see how excited he was.

Mina hesitated for a moment, and then reached out to hold his hand.

Nico looked surprised, but then he laced his fingers between hers. Together, they walked the rest of the way like that, talking about various options for what they could do instead of coffee, and finally settled on having coffee at Nico's apartment instead of a coffee shop, which made them both laugh.

"I don't have anything fancy," said Nico. "Just some sugar and milk if that hasn't expired already. But at least we'll be safe."

"That sounds perfect." Mina smiled.

The gated community came into view. At the entrance, a man asked and Niko for identification. He ducked into a little glass building that reminded Mina of a phone booth and called someone. She wondered if he was calling her professor. After a few moments, he returned their student badges, and let them on the grounds.

Professor Rosa's house wasn't far. And as Mina and Nico drew near, she saw her sitting outside on a porch swing. When she spotted Mina and Nico, Professor Rosa stood and waved.

Nico let go of Mina's hand and waved goodbye. Mina was a little disappointed that there wasn't a chance for a kiss goodbye.

"I'll see you tomorrow for coffee," he said, then walked away.

Professor Rosa waved Mina inside. "Come on in. Dinner's ready."

A man greeted them in the entry hallway. "Hello Mina, I'm Vincent." He spoke quietly, and Mina could tell, he was very shy.

Mina opened her bag and pulled out a small bakery box. "I brought some sugar cookies."

Vincent smiled and thanked her. He took the cookies and brought them into the dining room, where he set them on the table.

Professor Rosa motioned for Mina to take a seat. "We'll have dinner first, and then, I'll show you around the house."

"Sounds great, thank you," said Mina.

When the three of them sat down to eat, Mina noticed that Vincent was mostly quiet, but he looked over at Professor Rosa frequently. Mina wondered if there was something more between the two of them, and recognized the way that Vincent was looking at Professor Rosa as the way she had often looked at Nico back when she thought he was dating Autumn. It was like Vincent had feelings for her but didn't think he had a chance.

Mina wondered what it would be like to live with the two of them. She could tell Vincent had a kind soul. Even though he didn't talk much, everything he said was soft and polite, and he had a genuine smile that made his light up with joy.

The dinner wasn't as uncomfortable as Mina thought that it might be. Professor Rosa and Vincent made her feel more than welcome, and at the end of the night, she agreed to move in with them the following day.

Nico Fratelli

Being fired was the last thing Nico expected when he walked into Professor Rosa's office first thing Tuesday morning. She had emailed him the night before and looking back, Nico could see how she had hinted there was some bad news. He was hurt to have been fired from his TA position, but it wasn't like he needed the job or the work experience. Over his educational studies, he had done plenty of work for the music department in the past to build up a small resume before graduation. And he made enough money at the music shop to get by for the rest of the year.

When he asked Professor Rosa what had happened, she told him he would be too distracting for Mina.

Nico was shocked. He didn't know what to say to that. He didn't know if he should stand and leave, or if he needed to stay longer.

Professor Rosa explained, "When you have the kind of talent this girl does, you're indebted to the world. If she spends all of her time with you, she wouldn't create."

She rested her elbows on the table in a way that was probably meant to be casual, but in his viewpoint, it came off as almost menacing in the moment.

"I believe Mina has the potential to be added to history as one of the best contemporary composers in the world—of our time. You distract her, and your influence takes her focus away from where her real talent lies, in the orchestra."

Still in shock, and somewhat hurt by the accusation that he'd keep her from music, Nico said, "You can't make her choices for her."

"Mina doesn't know what she wants. She's only twenty years old. In twenty more years, she'll thank you for staying away."

Nico got up and left without another word, slamming the door behind him. But as he walked back home, he couldn't help but wonder if Professor Rosa was right. He had been spending a lot of time with Mina, and it was possible she was falling behind because of it.

There was only about an hour before Mina was supposed to go over to his apartment for coffee. Nico didn't want to still be angry when she got there but didn't have much time to sort through what had just happened.

Should I tell her? Nico was afraid Mina would feel as if she had to move out of Professor Rosa's house, and he didn't know where else she would go.

Ultimately, Nico knew he probably should tell Mina about what happened. But Mina's situation wasn't a regular one, and Nico thought it would be better off if she didn't know. Professor Rosa only wanted what was best for Mina, unlike Harris and Dustin, who wanted what was best for themselves.

A knock on the door signaled she had arrived. When he let her in, she had a big smile on her face. And soon, Nico forgot about all of his anger and stress.

"Hey, you look happy."

"I have something I want to show you," Mina said, handing Nico a few sheets of paper.

"What's this?" He took them from her.

"It's a little song I wrote, and I thought that you and your band might be interested in playing it." Mina blushed. "I know it's not great. But it's my first time writing something that's not meant for an orchestra.

Nico looked over the music and smiled. "No, this looks incredible. We were looking for some new things to play, too. Thank you."

In the back of his head, Nico wondered if this was what Professor Rosa was referencing earlier.

Had Mina shown this to her?

He knew Mina was working on composing for her orchestra class, and worried he really was talking her focus away from what should be her priority.

"How'd you find the time to do this?"

"I've just been doing so much composing for an orchestra lately, so I've been in a music-writing mindset, but there's only so many hours a day, I can think about violins and other stringed instruments without feeling like I'm going insane." Mina laughed.

"This looks seriously incredible." Nico read over the music again.

Mina blushed once more. "Thanks. It's not really a big deal."

Nico had known Mina was an incredible musician and had assumed that she was also good at composition because of the position Professor Rosa had given her, but he really had no idea exactly what she was capable of. It seemed like every time he learned something new about her, she became even more impressive.

"There's even a solo in there for a cello, well, if you were interested in something like that." A shy smile crossed her lips. "I haven't really heard you play except for the one band practice. But I thought . . . you don't have to, I mean . . ."

"No, seriously. This is incredible." He flipped through the sheets, locating the solo.

The song Mina had written was short, and the instrumental parts looked simple, but Nico could tell there was some complex thought behind the notes and couldn't wait to try it out. The lyrics were upbeat and lively, about watching the seasons turn, looking at the last explosion of color before snow covered everything up.

Not wanting to make Mina even more embarrassed, Nico set the sheets of paper on his table and started walking into the kitchen.

"Coffee?" He played the notes of the solo silently in his head, imagining playing the piece on his bass instead of a cello. He hoped she wouldn't mind.

Mina nodded. "Sugar and cream, if it's not expired."

"No, I checked this morning." Nico laughed. "It's still good."

He poured coffee into two mugs and brought out sugar packets and a carton of creamer for Mina. They sat down, cross-legged on the couch, facing each other.

Balancing his coffee on his knee, switching it to his other when it got too hot.

Across from him, Mina sipped her coffee, stealing little glances of him over the rim of the cup.

Nico cleared his throat. He knew he had to say something to Mina about his feelings, especially after the kiss just a few days before. They hadn't had a chance alone to talk since it had happened, but now Nico was even more conflicted after his talk with Professor Rosa. He knew Mina was graduating early, so she was swamped in classes, and she had already missed a whole week recovering from her abduction. He wondered if asking Mina to be his girlfriend would take her focus off where it needed to be.

But when he looked at her, he knew he had to say something. She was capable enough to have gotten herself to a successful place, and Nico had to trust, she knew how to manage her time and focus.

"So, I was wondering . . ." Nico started, but realized he hadn't yet thought out what he wanted to say. He took a sip of coffee to buy himself some time.

"About the kiss?"

Nico looked at her, shocked. She hid behind her mug again, taking another sip of coffee.

"Uh, yeah." Nico tugged on the end of his shirt even though it didn't need straightening. "Would you want to uhm . . . do that more?" Nico internally hit his head, wondering why he couldn't have found a better way to phrase it. "Not just kissing and stuff, I mean more . . ." He shook his head feeling like he'd put his foot in his mouth.

Mina laughed. "I think so, yeah."

Nico relaxed a bit, letting out a sigh of relief. "If you want, we can even go on a real date. You know when it's safe."

"I'd love that." Mina smiled.

Nico and Mina both took another sip of coffee, and it seemed to him, he wasn't the only one afraid to make the next move. After their first kiss, Nico knew Mina had feelings for him, but for some reason, he hadn't quite prepared himself for this moment. In the back of his head, he was still expecting her to say she didn't like him. So now, he that had what he wanted, he didn't know what to do next.

Mina set her coffee on the floor and looked at Nico.

Is she trying to kiss me? Nico thought. He slowly set his coffee on the floor next to hers.

Mina leaned forward and held his face between her hands. He closed his eyes, and her lips met his. Sweet coffee and a hit of creamer lingered on her lips and tongue. She looped her arms around his neck, drawing him in closer.

Mina pulled away. "Thank you." A dreamy gaze met his.

"For what?" A nervous chuckle passed his lips.

Mina blushed. "Just for making me so happy."

Nico pulled Mina into a tight hug. "In that case, thank you for making me happy, too."

He leaned back on the couch, bring Mina with him. For a while, he just stayed there in silence, enjoying the way her breaths slowed down to match his.

Mina broke the silence, "Can I ask you a question?"

Nico's heart raced. "Sure. You can ask me anything."

"It's not really related to, well, this." Mina gestured at Nico. "But I was wondering if you could actually do me a favor with my project."

"Of course." Nico drew in a deep breath, relishing the fresh lavender scent of her hair. "What is it?"

"I've been thinking about the song I'm working on. It's just, well, a little boring. I feel like everything I write has been done before, in some way."

Nico nodded, understanding completely. It was hard to be creative, especially when you were still finding your voice and style.

"I want to do something new. I've been working on a few things with Professor Rosa that are more traditional, but I'd like to end the concert on something more interesting. So, I'm working on a song that would incorporate different elements into the orchestra—something more modern to marry the new with the old."

Nico moved to play with Mina's hair as she talked, causing her to pause and close her eyes for a moment.

"I was thinking." She chewed on the corner of her mouth. "It might be a good idea for you if you and your band to play with the orchestra. I could compose a kind of hybrid song."

Nico paused to think about it. He wanted to help Mina with her project, and thought it sounded really interesting, but he also knew it might be hard to convince Robin and Luca to play something like this. It wasn't what they usually did. And any time he picked up a stringed instrument, they weren't crazy about it, but they seemed to tolerate it. This would be different from anything they had played. But Nico didn't want to turn down the opportunity to help Mina out.

"Yeah." Nico kissed her cheek. "That actually sounds really cool. I'm in."

Mina smiled. "Really?"

"I just have to convince the rest of the band first, but I'm sure they'll cave as long as I promise to buy them pizza."

"Thank you." Her eyes lit up. "I'm still working on the song. But I think I'll be able to get it to you by the end of the week—pending approval from Professor Rosa, of course."

"Take your time with it. I can wait."

After just a few more minutes, Mina sat up. She looked at the window and frowned.

"It's getting dark out. I don't want to go, but I should get home before it's too late."

Nico nodded. "I'll walk you."

Both Nico and Mina got up slowly and reluctantly pulled on their shoes and coats. Once outside the door, Mina reached down and took Nico's hand.

"Aren't you afraid Dustin will see?" Nico's gaze darted to every dark patch of scenery where someone could hide.

"I can't live my life in fear. Besides"—Mina shrugged—"you're my boyfriend now."

Mina Beth Lu

A block away from Professor Rosa's house, the flashing lights of an ambulance strobed.

"Oh, no. No. No." She ran, fearing the worst.

A thousand different scenarios whirled through her head, all of them involving something horrific Dustin might have done to Professor Rosa or Vincent.

It took less than a minute for Mina to run the rest of the way home. She arrived at the porch panting and watched as paramedics carried Vincent out on a stretcher, followed closely by Professor Rosa.

"What happened?" Mina asked, panicked.

Professor Rosa paused next to Mina on the steps. "I don't know." Her eyes were red from crying. "I think it was a heart attack. We're going to the hospital."

"Sylvia?" Vincent called for Professor Rosa with a weak voice.

"I'm right here." Professor Rosa followed the stretcher, then got into the ambulance.

In a matter of seconds, the ambulance had sped off to the hospital.

Mina and Nico were left alone on the porch. She tried to wrap her head around what had happened.

"It wasn't Dustin." Mina felt a little guilty that she was relieved.

"I know." Nico nodded. "I had the same thought at first."

Mina looked around at the empty street. "What should we do?"

"I don't know. Do you have Professor Rosa's phone number?"

Mina nodded.

"Then you should text her."

"And say what?"

"Maybe ask her to let you know when they have an update?"

"Good idea." Mina took out her phone and sent Professor Rosa a message.

"Do you want me to wait with you?" Nico seemed uneasy or nervous.

"Please." Mina took his hand in hers.

She led Nico through the already open front door, closing it tightly behind her, then she turned the deadbolt latch.

"Just in case," she said.

She plopped on the couch in the living room, and he joined her. Both sat in a nervous silence. Mina kept checking her phone, waiting to see if Professor Rosa had said anything.

It seemed like hours had passed with them waiting on any kind of news. Just as Mina started to think they weren't going to find anything out tonight, she got a text from Professor Rosa.

"She said they're in the ICU, and they're keeping him for a few days." Mina, still worried, felt a sliver of relief.

"Was it a heart attack?" Nico asked.

"Yeah." She nodded. "She's asking if I can bring her some things because she wants to spend the night with him in the hospital. Do you have time to help?"

"Of course, I can borrow my uncle's car drive us over." He headed for the door. It will take me about ten minutes to get to my house on foot, and then I'll drive back. It should take me what, about fifteen minutes."

She saw him to the door. "Thanks for doing this. It means a lot to me."

"Hey, I'm just glad I can help." He kisses her on the cheek, then turned to leave. "Be sure to lock up while I'm gone."

Once inside, Mina engaged the deadbolt. She rushed around the house gathering the supplies Professor Rosa had asked for, including a blanket, food, and her toothbrush. By the time Mina had finished packing, Nico returned with the car.

The hospital was only a five-minute drive from the house. When they got there, she and Nico entered through the emergency room. Mina went up to the desk and talked to the nurse, who let them to the ICU waiting room, but it was empty.

"I guess she's with Vincent." She sent a text, letting her know she and Nico had arrived.

"Let's take a seat in the corner over there." Nico pointed. "We'll be out of the way and still see the ICU door when it opens."

A few minutes later, Professor Rosa came out to meet them in the waiting area.

"How is he?" Mina rose.

"He's finally falling asleep now, they put him on some pain medication." She adjusted the sweater she wore. "If I had been home when it happened . . ." Her voice cracked. "Maybe he would have gotten medical attention sooner."

"He's okay though, and that's what matters." Mina gave

her a hug and handed her the bag with the supplies she had asked for.

Nico stood to the side, watching hospital staff walking up and down the hallway.

Mina wondered why he seemed so uncomfortable, but she figured it was because he didn't know Professor Rosa or Vincent that well.

"Oh, Mina, he knew it was a heart attack. He tried to call me, but I didn't pick up the phone," said Professor Rosa. "I was lucky, I was already on my way home. He just didn't want to go outside. He's too afraid."

The doors opened, and a nurse peeked around the frame. "Professor Rosa." She locked gazes with Mina's instructor. "He's asking for you."

"Come with me." Professor Rosa took her by the hand. "He was worried about you."

"About me?" She was surprised by her words. "Why?"

"He didn't want you coming home to an empty house." She wiped a tear away. "He was worried you'd be afraid to stay there all alone."

"I feel safe with the fenced in community. And the guards at the front entry points, card everyone they don't know, which is nice." She patted the woman's shoulder.

"I should go." Professor Rosa's gaze rose eye level. "Will you come in for a bit and say hello?"

She glanced over her shoulder at Nico.

"Go. I'll wait here for you." He gestured for her to escort the professor.

The nurse kept a steady pace down the corridor. ICU rooms sat on both sides: odd numbers on the left and even on the right.

From outside Room 7, Mina heard Vincent weakly call out, "Sylvia?"

"Thank you, Mina." Professor Rosa hurried inside the room. "Yes, I'm here, Vincent."

"I was worried that you had left." Vincent's voice shook.

"I wouldn't leave you alone." She tugged on Mina's hand. "Look who stopped by."

"Hello, Vincent." Mina gave a little wave.

"Oh, I'm so happy to see you." A weak smile touched his lips. "You're a breath of sunshine in this drab room." He held out a hand to her.

Professor Rosa sat the bag with the blanket and other supplies on a chair that would later recline into a bed.

"Did they say when you might come home?" She sat on the edge of his bed and held his hand. It was cool to the touch, and the tips of his fingers had calloused like hers and Nico's, from years of playing stringed instruments.

"Not for a few days." He patted her hand. "So, will you feed Mr. Whiskers?"

"Of course." Mina nodded.

"He likes his meal worms in the morning, not at night."

"I'll text her the information, Vincent," said Professor Rosa.

Mr. Whiskers, a barred tiger salamander, was his pride and joy. So, she felt both honored and nervous he had asked her to care for him.

Observing their interaction, Mina wondered if Professor Rosa knew how much Vincent loved her.

"I better head out before it gets any later." Mina rose. "And don't worry about a thing. I'll even send you some Mr. Whisker selfies."

The last comment got a little chuckle from Vincent.

"Night." She made her way to the door.

"Text me when you get home," said Professor Rosa.

"I will." She stepped into the hall.

Mina was tempted to wait outside the room to see if he would confess his feelings for her, but then thought it was best to give them some privacy. Plus, Nico was waiting.

As she walked away, she heard Vincent say, "I love you."

Not wanting to eavesdrop any more than she already had, Mina walked of the ICU unit and into the waiting room, where she found Nico texting his aunt and uncle.

On the way home, Mina held one of Nico's hands as he drove. When he dropped her off, he walked her to the door.

"Call me if you need me. I have my uncle's car until Vincent is out of the hospital. So, if you need anything, let me know." He leaned over and kissed her.

Nico Fratelli

Nico sat by the door of the music shop, waiting impatiently for Robin and Luca to show up for practice.

On the one day they decide to show up late, we actually have something important to do, Nico thought, rolling his eyes.

When he saw them walking up to the door, he threw it open and motioned them inside. "You're late."

"Relax, dude." Robin squeezed between Nico and the doorframe. "You'll still have time to impress your girlfriend, don't worry."

Nico turned his head away. He was embarrassed Robin had guessed the reason why he was so anxious for them to show up on time.

Mina was waiting for them in the practice room. They had practiced almost every day since she had given him the final version of the music she had written, and Mina had made it to every one of their sessions to watch. Nico had gotten comfortable with singing around her and was even more excited than anxious to be performing such an important concert. If it didn't go well, Mina might not be able to graduate.

Nico was confident that everything would turn out well. Life had been almost quiet recently, and he was starting to think that Dustin and Harris had left town entirely. There hadn't been any talk of sightings. The drama had worn off, so the community was starting to forget all about what had happened.

The band got set up and started to play. Usually, in the past practice sessions, Mina would stop them and provide notes or suggestions. This time, she didn't have anything to say. So, together as a unified group, he played through the music perfectly a few times with the guys.

"That sounded great." Mina clapped her hands.

Over the last couple of days, Robin and Luca had started to get frustrated with Nico about his insistence that they keep practicing, even though they had the music down perfectly.

There are only a few days left until the performance. He sighed.

Nico really didn't want to let Mina down. He also knew if he pushed his friends too hard, they might not forgive him so easily after the performance was over.

"Should we call it a little early today?" Nico glanced around the room.

"Thank, God," Luca joked. "I thought I was going to die back here."

Robin and Luca packed up quickly as if worried Nico or Mina would change their minds. He followed the guys to the front of the shop to lock the door behind them when they left. But when he got to the door, Nico paused, confused.

"What's wrong?" Robin bumped into him.

"It's unlocked." Nico stared at the door. "I could have sworn I locked it earlier. . ."

Luca shrugged. "Must have forgotten."

Nico looked around the shop nervously.

"I didn't hear anyone come in, and it was only unlocked for what, thirty minutes?" Robin looked over Luca's shoulder.

"Yeah," agreed Nico, trying to shrug off his nerves. "It's probably okay."

Robin and Luca walked out, and Nico double checked he had locked the door behind them this time.

A blood-curdling scream sounded from the back room.

Nico jumped and ran to Mina faster than he thought was possible.

Mina was backed into the far corner of the room, away from the door. Dustin was slowly walking toward her, holding a gallon of gasoline.

"Stop," yelled Nico.

Dustin turned around and laughed. "What are you gonna do? Sing about it?"

Nico grabbed his phone from his pocket, and the screen came alive. An image of Autumn, and his last message to her popped up.

"Uh-huh." Dustin shook his head. "I wouldn't do that if I were you." He held up a book of matches. "Put it on the floor."

One hand in the air, he kneeled, hit the call button, then turned the phone face down on the floor, hoping the light from the screen wouldn't give him away.

Please pick up, Autumn. Please.

A puddle of gasoline covered the floor, and Mina was standing in the middle of it. To make matters worse, she was next to the helium tank used to fill balloons during store events. And if memory served him, it was still more than half full.

She looked at Nico with panicked eyes. If Dustin dropped a match, Mina would be right in the middle of the explosion.

He had to buy time and hope for the best—that Autumn would answer her phone.

"What are you doing here?" Nico rose, hands in the air.

"Taking care of some loose ends." Dustin reached into the box of matches and pulled one out.

Holding the match, he toyed with both Nico and Mina. Mina's crying seemed to delight him. Dustin was enjoying the deadly game he was playing.

"When I'm done here, you'll have nothing left." He ran the match along the side of the box just not hard enough to light the match. "Do you hear me?"

Mina whimpered, tears running down her face.

Dustin struck the match again, this time,

"Wait!" Nico felt helpless. If he tried to charge at Dustin, he would just light the match and drop it. There was no way Nico would be able to get to Mina on time.

Glass shattered in the front of the shop. Seconds later, Autumn burst through the doors, panting, and with the steel base of a music stand in her hands—held like a bat. She looked at Dustin like she wasn't surprised to see him.

"The police are right behind me." Autumn rose the impromptu weapon over her shoulder as if preparing to windup for a swing. "I suggest that you leave now."

Nico stared at her, shocked.

Dustin paused for a moment, dropped the empty gas canister and the unlit matches, then ran out the back door.

"How did you know he was here?" Nico staggered back a few steps. "Did you get my call?"

"Call? No." Autumn ran to move the matches away from the gas.

Mina took a few shaky steps away from the wall toward Nico, and he drew her into a comforting hug.

"I was on my way to the drugstore for some candy, and I thought I saw Dustin on the street. So, I followed as quickly as I could."

"When did you call the police?" Nico wasn't sure if Mina was shaking, or if it was him. "Are they on their way?"

Autumn laughed, which really confused Nico.

"No, that part was a lie." She lowered the music stand rod, setting the base back on the floor. "I didn't call the police. I wasn't even positive it was Dustin until I saw him here."

"Y-you saved my life." Mina swallowed hard.

"It's no big deal," said Autumn, uncomfortable with the attention. "What is it with that guy and fire, anyway?"

Still wrapped in Nico's arms, Mina asked, "Shouldn't we call the police now?"

"Oh shoot, yeah." Autumn grabbed her phone, then she made a face. "Hey, says here, I have a missed call from you." She shot a glance at Nico.

"Yeah, you were the last person I talked to on the phone, so when I set my phone on the floor, I called you. That's why I thought you were here."

Nico grabbed several bags of kitty litter, which the shop often uses to remove moisture from instruments and poured them over the gasoline.

The police arrived and searched the area. Not long after, his aunt and uncle walked into the music store.

"Are you kids okay?" Uncle Harold entered first, followed by Nico's aunt.

"Yeah," shouted Autumn. "We're in the back."

His aunt and uncle rounded the corner. A new wave of tears escaped Mina's eyes.

"I'm so sorry," she said between sobs. "This is all my fault."

"No. It's not." Harold grabbed a bag of cat litter, and helped Nico stop the spread of a trail of gas snaking its way to a shelf of supplies. "None of this is your fault."

"Come here, dear," Aunt Eden opened her arms. "Now, don't you fret none."

"Did they get him?" Harold stood next to Nico, relief on his face.

"Not yet." Nico shook his head. "But they said they'd keep searching the area."

A few firemen entered the room with an officer.

"My name is Officer Sánchez, and this is Lt. Rick Mayweather." The officer motioned to the fireman in full gear.

"Once forensics and the fire marshal are done collection evidence."—Lt. Mayweather held out a hand to Uncle Harold —"my crew and I will get this cleaned up in no time."

"Sounds like a plan." Uncle Harold walked away with the officer, who needed more information on the building.

Nico was still shocked over what happened—was still happening. He had just been thinking about how lucky he and Mina had been since they hadn't heard anything from Dustin for a while.

He rejoined the girls and waited for his turn to give his statement. After the police had taken everyone's statement, the detective in charge approached their little group.

"Miss Lu." Detective Fontana handed Nico a card, then he turned his attention to Mina. "I don't recommend you return home, alone. Is there anywhere you can go?"

Mina looked over at Nico. "Would it be weird if I asked to stay with you? I don't want to involve Professor Rosa and Vincent in this. And they're not even home right now."

"Of course." Nico was glad Mina trusted him enough to keep her safe.

"Good," said Detective Fontana. "I've assigned Officer Sánchez to keep watch."

"Thank you," was all Mina managed to say.

Officer Sánchez drove them to Nico's apartment, and stayed parked outside to watch over the building, so they could sleep without fear of another attack, but Nico wasn't sure he'd be able to sleep knowing Dustin was still on the loose.

Once he and Mina were settled in his garage apartment over his aunt's and uncle's house, he turned to her. She looked exhausted, as if she hadn't slept in days.

"You can take the bed. I'll stay on the couch tonight." He grabbed a pillow off his bed.

Mina looked at the ground and sighed. "Actually, would you mind staying with me? J-just to sleep?"

Nico nodded and kissed her forehead. "Of course."

He led Mina into his bedroom, then rummaged through his drawers.

"Here." He handed her a shirt and sweats. "They're gonna be big, but they won't smell like gas."

"Thanks."

"Oh, and there are clean towels in the linen closet." He turned the light on for her in the bathroom. "Leave your stuff over there, he pointed to the top of the plastic hamper, and tomorrow, we can wash it at my aunt's place."

"Okay." She entered the bathroom, then shut the door.

Not even ten minutes later, she was dressed and brushing out her hair.

"I'm really tired." A yawn escaped her lips.

Once in bed, Nico wrapped his arm around her, holding her close, and soon, Mina's steady breaths let him know she was asleep.

Nico stayed awake, listening to every creaking floorboard and the sounds of the neighborhood, half expecting Dustin to make an appearance. But after a few hours, Nico finally relaxed enough to fall asleep.

Mina Beth Lu

Mina was more than positive she'd throw up. She struggled to calm down, taking deep, slow breaths. It was only fifteen minutes before the concert—her concert—was about to start.

People in the audience took their seats, and murmurs sounded all around the area.

She was almost certain that Dustin would make an appearance tonight. Worry ate at her.

Glancing out into the crowd, her gaze rested on Nico's aunt and uncle, then Autumn, who were sitting in the center of the front row. She searched the faces, some familiar, other not, and saw Detective Fontana and Officer Sánchez. There were police in the audience, some in their dressed-blue uniforms, and others in plain clothing.

Even with all the protection in place, she couldn't shake the feeling that Dustin was lurking about, waiting to do something. She feared his actions would put the entire orchestra and audience in danger. Earlier in the day, she had wanted to cancel the concert altogether. But Detective

Fontana had assured her, he and the officers assigned to her case, would be keeping a close watch and would stop Dustin if he decided to make an appearance.

Plus, if Mina called off the concert, she wouldn't earn a graded for her work, which would mean, she wouldn't be able to graduate this year.

Mina took one last deep breath, then opened the backstage door. Just as she was about to walk in, she heard someone running down the hallway. Panicked, Mina jumped, ready to run. But when she looked at the person who was running, it wasn't Dustin or Harris.

"Wait," a female police officer called out.

Mina shut the door and stepped back into the hallway.

"What is it?" Mina asked, fearing something terrible had happened.

The officer paused just long enough to catch her breath. "We caught them." A smile of satisfaction grew on the woman's face.

"What?" Mina was shocked and didn't really believe that this was happening.

"A student reported a sighting on campus a few minutes ago, and since we were already here, we were able to catch them before they got away."

"Both of them?" Mina couldn't believe her ears.

"Yes, we've got them in custody. You shouldn't have to worry anymore." The officer put a reassuring hand on Mina's shoulder.

"What were they doing here?"

"They had a large amount of gasoline and a lighter. We think they were planning on setting the stage on fire, but we aren't certain yet."

Mina didn't know what to say. She had spent the whole day worrying about what Dustin might do and didn't even have time to worry about the performance. Now, with them in custody, she felt a whole other wave of anxiety.

"Good luck on your performance." The police officer smiled at her. "We'll contact you when we have more information, but for now, just know, you're safe."

"Thank you." A wave of relief hit her, and she crossed her arms over her chest as if hugging herself.

The officer turned and walked quickly back down the hall.

Mina looked at the door, trying to settle her nerves before walking in.

The door swung open, and she jumped, but relaxed when she saw Nico walking out.

"Did you hear the news?" A smile grew on his face, brightening his eyes.

"I did." She nodded. "An officer just told me they were in custody—captured on campus."

"It's over." He hugged her.

"I'm relieved, but I'm also, well . . ."

"What?"

"Nervous about tonight. I want to do well."

"You're ready for this. Actually, you were born for this. Music is in soul."

She grinned, then hugged him again.

"Everyone's seated," he said. "Let's do this, okay?"

Mina nodded. Nico took her hand and together they walked toward the stage. Robin and Luca were waiting to the side. Their song wasn't on until last.

The curtains opened, making a faint swishing sound.

Mina walked out onto the stage, and a round of applause greeted her.

The stage lights blocked the audience from view, but it sounded like almost every seat had been taken up. Instead of being nervous, Mina grew more confident with each step she took.

She reached the center of the stage, bowed to the audience, then turned and smiled at the orchestra. Mina raised the baton in her hand—a gift from Vincent and Professor Rosa—counting off a tempo, and then the seated members started to play.

As she was conducting the orchestra through the songs, Mina forgot about Harris and Dustin, about the fear she had been living with for the past few months. There were only the notes on the pages, and her breath in tempo with the music.

After the first few songs, she paused, and let the orchestra receive applause before she introduced the last song.

"For my last composition, I wanted to do something a little bit differently." Mina motioned for Nico, Robin, and Luca to come onto the stage. "I wanted a way to combine the different aspects of my life and my interests together. So, I came up with a little song that's unlike anything that I have ever written before. I hope you all enjoy it."

Mina smiled at the audience, and they clapped. She turned back around to the musicians, gave them a tempo, then started the song.

It seemed like every different part of the song just flowed together naturally, as if Nico's band and the orchestra were meant to be heard together. Mina hadn't had very many chances to hear it all together because of scheduling conflicts, so when Nico stood in the back with a bass instead of off to the side with a cello, her eyes widened in surprise.

When it came time for his solo instrumental, which would lead into his vocal piece, she waited with bated breath. She directed the orchestra players to soften their sounds on a decrescendo.

Her eyes focused on Nico, and his fingers flowed over the strings of the base, strumming with a seductive quality that drew her eye. Clear, earthy notes found her ears, bringing a smile to her lips. Sliding his bow over the strings, the rich intonation of the notes, soothed to her soul. She watched, mesmerized by the way he held the instrument as he played. It was as if he were caressing each note.

Eyes closed, he continued to play, swaying to the rhythm of the piece. The way he held the instrument, made her long to be in his arms, where she felt safe, loved, and cherished. When he set the bass down and made his way to the microphone off to the side of where she conducted, he winked at her, making her heart flutter.

She counted off the entrance of his band, and they hit the notes right on beat.

Nico held the microphone stand and released the first waves of notes. The full, rich sound of his tenor voice filled the auditorium. Everything was perfect, she couldn't have asked for anything more from the band, orchestra, or Nico.

When the last note ended, the musicians stood, then bowed to the audience, who was still clapping a few minutes later when the last musician had filed off the stage.

Professor Rosa had set up a formal reception in the common room, and Mina followed a small crowd over. When she got there, Professor Rosa wrapped her arms around her, giving her a big hug.

"Wow, that was incredible," said Professor Rosa.

"Thank you. So, did I pass?" Mina asked, only half joking.

Professor Rosa laughed. "You went above and beyond with this assignment, Mina. I was worried you wouldn't have time to accomplish everything, but I clearly underestimated your focus and your courage. It was my honor to have worked with you this past semester."

Mina smiled and looked away, not used to having this much praise.

"And yes, you did pass," Professor Rosa added. "I'm sorry to leave you in a rush, but I have to get back to the house with Vincent."

Is Vincent here? Mina wondered, looking around.

She was shocked to find he had been standing next to

Professor Rosa the whole time. He had been so quiet, Mina hadn't noticed him among all the commotion in the room.

"Vincent." She hugged him. "Thank you so much for coming."

"It was my pleasure to be able to hear the final result of all your hard work," said Vincent with a warm smile.

"Well, I guess we'll see you at home tonight, then." Professor Rosa gave Mina one last hug before she and Vincent headed out.

Once they were gone, Mina looked around for Nico. She spotted him standing by the door, talking to Autumn.

"Hey," Mina called out, walking toward them.

"Wow, Mina." Autumn, wearing a dress, brought laughter to bubble on Mina's lips. "I had no idea you were so talented. The concert was amazing."

Mina blushed. "Thank you."

Nico looked around. "Seems like just about the whole school came out for this."

"Yeah," Mina said, wide-eyed. "It's a bit overwhelming right now."

"Do you want me to walk you home?"

Mina took a second to decide. She didn't want to leave so soon, but she was so exhausted from the long day.

"I'd like that." Mina leaned against him.

"Bye, guys." Autumn headed toward the food table. "Free food awaits."

She and Nico said their goodbyes to some of the performers. She was surprised to find his band still in the common room, talking to a few of her classmates.

Outside and away from the chatter, Mina felt peaceful for the first time in a long while. She was able to let go of all the pent-up stress over the last several weeks and found she was even feeling more energetic once they had left the building.

Nico held her hand as they walked, and he even matched the tempo of her footsteps.

Mina let out a sigh of relief, glad she didn't have to be constantly looking over her shoulder for danger.

Nico stopped walking suddenly, and Mina turned to look at him.

"What is it?" She asked, a surge of worry crept into her mind, making her wonder if she had forgotten or missed something.

"Nothing." Nico drew her into a tender embrace. "I just . . ."

He leaned over and kissed Mina, running his fingers through her hair.

"I think . . ." he said. "I'm in love with you."

Mina's heart raced, and for a moment, she thought she might be dreaming. After all, Dustin and Harris had been caught, the concert went perfectly without a hitch or hiccup, and now this. Nothing could be more perfect that this moment—here and now.

"Is this real?" Mina whispered. "Am I awake?"

Nico laughed softly. "Yes, you're awake."

Mina stood on her toes and kissed him.

"I love you, too," she whispered in his ear.

THE END

ABOUT THE AUTHOR

Evie Ralston is a North American author of fairy tales and contemporary women's fiction. She travels the United States with her husband, children, and cat, Cleo.